"We're Driving Forever, Bryan!"

With a splintering crack, the car burst out the back of the garage.

Back on the street, they took the next corner so sharply that two of the tires lifted high in the air.

"Wheeeeee!" the girl cried.

The Cataluna bumped down. Fishtailed. Then zoomed ahead.

Straight for a group of high school kids playing touch football in the street.

I can't stop, Bryan realized. I'm going to run them down!

Pounding on the silent horn, Bryan uttered a long scream of horror.

Gleeful laughter from the girl.

"Stop laughing!" Bryan cried. "Who are you? Who?"

Books by R. L. Stine

Available from ARCHWAY Paperbacks

FEAR STREET®
R·L·STINE

The Evil Moon

A Parachute Press Book

AN ARCHWAY PAPERBACK
Published by POCKET BOOKS
New York   London   Toronto   Sydney   Tokyo   Singapore

This book is a work of fiction. Names, characters, places and
incidents are products of the author's imagination or are used
fictitiously. Any resemblance to actual events or locales or persons,
living or dead, is entirely coincidental.

AN ARCHWAY PAPERBACK *Original*

 An Archway Paperback published by
POCKET BOOKS, a division of Simon & Schuster Inc.
1230 Avenue of the Americas, New York, NY 10020

ISBN: 0-671-89433-1

First Archway Paperback printing August 1995

10 9 8 7 6 5 4 3 2 1

FEAR STREET is a registered trademark of
Parachute Press, Inc.

AN ARCHWAY PAPERBACK and colophon are
registered trademarks of Simon & Schuster Inc.

Cover art by Don Brautigam

Printed in the U.S.A.

IL 7+

prologue

“Whoever heard of a Cataluna?”

"Who makes it?"

"Who cares? It's a great-looking car."

Two boys circled slowly around the sleek white car in Denny's used car lot. High above the lot hung a full moon. The moon shone down on the car like a spotlight. Its metal body gleamed.

"What do you think they want for it?" asked Matt Perkins.

"Whatever they're asking, it's more than we've got," his friend Chris answered. He slid his hand along the smooth curves of the car's hood.

"Yeah, I know, but . . ." Matt pulled up the collar of his denim jacket. The cold air still found its way down his neck. "Check this out," he said. He gestured to the long line of used cars. "This is the only car on the lot that doesn't have a price soaped on the windshield. Now, why is that?"

Chris stood taller than Matt and he had more muscle. But Chris's round face made him appear younger than his friend. He flipped his head to get the long hair out of his eyes. "Maybe it's not for sale, Matt," he replied. He sounded bored with the question. "Man, if *I* had a car like this, I sure wouldn't sell it." He traced a finger across the car's silver hood ornament. A statue of a pretty girl, her arms modestly crossed in front of her.

"Hey!" Matt exclaimed suddenly.

"What?"

"You're not going to believe this. The keys are in the car."

Chris gaped at his friend. "Get out of here!"

Matt smiled. "See for yourself."

Chris trotted around to the driver's side window. He peered in. Then he glanced around the lot. Plastic pennants—red, white, and blue—flapped in the cool night breeze. No one in sight. The lot had closed hours ago.

Chris grinned at Matt. He held out his hands palm up. Matt slapped both hands. "Let's go," Chris urged.

"Whoa. You sure?"

"Hey—why not? We'll bring it back in an hour. Who will know the difference? I want to feel how this baby handles."

The leather seats glowed red as blood. When the two boys climbed into the car, the warm, dark smell of leather enveloped them, as if they had slid inside a glove.

"Smell that," Matt murmured.

"Whoa! Not bad!"

Chris turned the ignition key. The car purred to life. He glanced at Matt. Then he guided the white sports car around the lot. He drove slowly at first, afraid of scratching such a gorgeous car. The car handled beautifully, reacting to the slightest turns of the wheel. "It can read my mind," Chris whispered.

Metal poles ringed most of the lot, the poles spaced closely together to prevent anyone from driving off with a car. Chris and Matt had walked between those poles, no problem. But the only way to drive a car off the lot was through the locked front gate.

A gate someone had left open.

"Tonight must be our lucky night," Chris declared. He pulled out onto the street.

"You can say that again," Matt agreed.

"Tonight must be our lucky night."

They both laughed.

Chris turned left. As they drove past the closed Exxon station, Matt leaned forward and turned on the radio. A screeching Aerosmith song boomed out of the speakers in front and back. Chris powered down the windows. He and Matt shouted out the words to the song. They started to relax and really have fun.

The car pushed sixty when it crossed Fear Street. Deserted at this hour.

"Having fun, boys?"

A woman's voice, low and teasing. Chris and Matt stopped singing.

"Who said that?" Matt asked.

"Must have come from the radio," Chris replied with a laugh. He turned the radio off. "These things pick up all kinds of CB broadcasts. And now, you know, with cellular phones, the airwaves are so jammed it's—"

"Oh, come on. You can go faster than this!" the voice whispered in their ears.

Matt spun around and peered into the backseat. Empty. He turned back. "This is so weird," he muttered.

Chris didn't answer.

"Hey, slow down," Matt warned.

"I can't!" Chris cried.

Chris didn't even have his foot on the gas pedal. But the car sped faster and faster. The strange woman's voice started laughing in his ears.

Up ahead the light turned yellow. Then red. A Lexus raced toward the intersection. "Chris, stop!" Matt yelled.

Chris slammed on the brakes. Nothing happened.

He couldn't stop.

The car was going to smash into them!

A horn screeched.

Tires wailed.

Chris burst through the intersection. "We missed it!" he shouted.

"Aren't we having fun, boys? What's that? You want to go even faster? Okay!"

Faster.

They were both screaming now.

The car veered left. Right. The sharp turns threw

them against the doors. Chris spun the wheel. They sped up the on ramp to the highway doing seventy.

Eighty.

But the yellow road signs warned SHARP CURVE AHEAD.

And the white sports car drove straight. Straight as a ruler.

Chris yanked his door open. "Jump!" he shrieked. "Matt, jump!"

Cold night air blasted into the car. The dotted white line appeared as a solid white blur beneath Chris's feet.

He leaped.

So did Matt.

The two boys flew out onto the highway. The pavement rushed up and struck them with incredible force.

They both rolled over a few times. Then lay still.

They didn't see the big truck rounding the curve, roaring toward them.

The boys lay still. Unconscious. Two lumps on the dark road.

An air horn blasted. The truck driver hit his brakes.

Not in time.

Bump. Bump.

Bump, bump. The truck's middle tires hit.

Bump, bump. The rear tires.

The big rig squealed to a stop. The driver pulled over to the side of the road. He jumped down from the cab and hurried back along the weedy shoulder of the highway.

The highway stood quiet. The rasp of crickets and

the faint hum of power lines provided the only sounds. The driver hiked eighty yards.

Did I hit a deer? he wondered.

Then he found the flattened, blood-soaked bodies of the boys. The tires had missed the first boy's head. Blue eyes stared up at him lifelessly from a round, babyish face. And a few yards away . . .

The truck driver bent over double, started to vomit.

Then something made him lift his gaze.

A white car sat on the side of the road.

Without a dent or a scratch.

The headlights pointed straight ahead.

"It's staring at me," the driver muttered.

Those two boys weren't the first victims of the strange white car.

I was.

Strange as it may seem, my suffering began three hundred years ago. In the long, dark history of the Cataluna, I am the only survivor. I've waited centuries to tell my story, and now it is time.

My story begins in the small New England colony of West Hampshire in 1698. . . .

September. A dark and dreary afternoon. An icy wind blew through the colony. The clouds hung low. You could tell another storm was coming. Who knew if we would survive it?

We had endured a harsh year. The animals lay dying. The crops were poor. The whole colony seemed to be cursed. . . .

part

1

West Hampshire Colony
1698

chapter

1

Catherine Hatchett, fifteen, peered longingly through the open window into the school. She stayed close to the wall, hidden to one side of the window frame. If the teacher spotted her, she would find herself in all kinds of trouble for disrupting class. More trouble. The last thing she needed.

"Amo, Amas, Amat," droned Master Porter, waving his hand through the air.

Around him on log benches sat the younger boys, repeating his every word. They studied Latin. Catherine spotted two five-year-olds. These young students could already read Latin, English, French, or Gothic letters.

Once Catherine had borrowed a boy's hornbook.

Fascinated, she peered through the thin sheet of yellowish horn. The alphabet and Lord's Prayer were printed on the sheet of paper beneath.

But Catherine's parents caught her studying the hornbook. Instead of an education, she had received a whipping.

All day long Catherine learned—nothing. Day after day she was expected to do the same dull chores around the house. It was not fair!

Now her eyes shifted to the far wall of the classroom. Pegs had been hammered into the walls. Boards lay on the pegs to make desks for the older scholars. They sat facing away from the teacher. Catherine could recognize the two handsome brothers Joseph and William Parker, even from the back.

"Hic, Haec . . ." A short, nervous, redheaded boy named Charles Foster conjugated his Latin verbs. Or tried to.

"Hic, Haec . . ." repeated Master Porter. "Continue."

"Hic, Haec . . ." Charles began again, obviously stuck.

Master Porter slapped his switch against his palm. "You are wasting precious time, Charles. There is but little time left in our day. *Hic, Haec . . ."*

"Hoc," said Catherine, without thinking. She covered her mouth in horror as all heads turned toward the window. She heard the students giggle.

At least she had blurted out the correct answer. But that gave Catherine small comfort. She felt certain Master Porter would catch her now.

Two of the younger boys began kicking at the dusty floor. They stirred up quite a cloud. Master Porter charged around the room with his switch. Ready to hand out punishment.

Catherine felt sorry for the boys who would be hit. But at least the teacher had been distracted from punishing *her*. She pressed against the wall of the school, breathing hard. You must be more careful, Catherine scolded herself. Her parents were already so angry with her. The rest of the colony, too.

Inside the classroom Master Porter restored order quickly. He led the entire class in the final prayer. Catherine hurried away along the dirt path. As she walked, she nervously tucked her shiny brown hair back under her white cap. It kept falling back out.

She heard boys yelling. Class had been dismissed. The boys would be running this way. She tried not to look back.

A young boy flew past on her left. *"Hic, Haec, Hoc!"* the boy shouted, pulling her arm hard. It hurt.

She shook her fist at him as he ran on. But now several more boys marched behind her on the path. She could feel them at her heels. She forced herself not to glance back. She lifted her long dark skirt with both hands so she could move faster.

"So, Bad Luck Catherine wants to come to school with the boys," chanted one boy in a singsong voice.

"She wants to get us all in trouble!"

"School is not for girls!"

She could no longer resist. She stopped short and stared down at the boys. "Do you think girls should not be allowed an education as well as boys? Hmm? Answer me. Do you think a girl enjoys having her mind go idle with nothing to challenge her? Do you?"

The boys stared at her with impish faces.

"Do you see the terrible boredom a girl suffers when all she may do is sew or cook or clean?" she demanded.

The boys laughed as if she had told them a joke. It had been a mistake for her to stop. Now she found herself in the middle of the stream of boys coming from the school. They had all heard her angry words. And they all joined in the laughter.

"Catherine," called a boy. "My father says your bad luck killed our pig."

"Get her!" cried another boy.

"Bad luck! Bad luck!"

Several boys raced toward her. She couldn't help it.

Catherine ran. Her long hair broke free of her cap. She reached up to hold it in, but that slowed her down. So did her skirt. Boys in their breeches could easily catch her.

An older boy, John North, darted ahead of her and blocked her way. He shoved her backward. "If you think you are as good as a boy, prove it." He shoved her harder. "Wrestle me."

"I do not want to wrestle you, John, I only want to—"

12

He pushed her again. The boys formed a ring around them. A ring of grinning, hateful faces.

John North grabbed her by the waist and threw her down. A cry of excitement went up from the boys. John pounced on top of her, pinning her arms.

She felt sharp stones grinding into her back and head. She screamed. Tried to twist away. She pushed the boy off, rolling on top of him. He grabbed her by the hair, yanking hard.

She raised a fist to strike him. But somebody caught her hand and pulled her to her feet.

"Get the hatchet," one boy called. "The hatchet for Hatchett!"

"Chop off her head!"

She felt her rage grow. She couldn't believe the boys had so much hatred inside them. And all of it directed at her. What had she done to deserve this?

She turned her back on them and stomped away. They followed, still taunting her. She struggled to hold back the tears.

Don't let them see you cry! she ordered herself. But when she wiped her face with the back of her hand, she felt tears mixed in with the dirt.

She stopped short, bent down, and scooped up a rock. She turned and held the rock high over her head. "Stay back now or I will throw it. I promise I will."

The sight of her holding the rock stopped the boys for a moment. But only a moment. Then they laughed and plunged forward.

"I am warning you!" she cried.

She threw the rock hard into the crowd. It struck a

boy in the head. The boy cried out, slumping to the ground.

Stunned silence. Nobody moved or spoke.

The boy lay still, his face gone pale as the belly of a toad. Then Catherine recognized him. Charles. The nervous boy with the red hair.

"You killed Charles!" a boy cried out. "You killed him! You killed him!"

chapter

2

Catherine covered her mouth with her hands. But she couldn't contain her horror. Had she really killed the boy?

Yes! The boy lay dead.

And now the colony would hang her. Tonight she would feel the bristly rope tighten around her thin neck. Choking out her last breath.

Charles suddenly sat up. He laughed.

William Parker pointed at Catherine. "She's all red!"

"She really thought she killed him!" Joseph Parker yelled.

"Fool!"

"And she thinks she can learn in school with *us!*"

A loud sob escaped Catherine. The boys laughed harder. She turned and ran along the dirt path through the woods.

Through the town square. Past the meeting house with its wooden steeple and bell. Past the stocks, the pillory, and the whipping post. Places of punishment for those who committed crimes.

She shuddered. Here she had once watched a man's flesh branded with a hot iron. He had been caught stealing another man's chickens. He would be marked with the crime for life.

She ran faster, although the boys no longer chased her. She dashed between two houses. Raced past Edmund Parker's house. Home to those two handsome boys, Joseph and William. She didn't pause. She ran past the Parkers' fenced-in garden. The cabbage patch brown and dry. Past the Tyler house. Past two sickly cows grazing on the patches of grass in the road. The cows slowly lifted their heads and stared at her darkly as she ran by.

Even the cows hate me! she thought.

She ran on. Past the well where several women of the colony had gathered. All wore long dresses, caps, and white aprons. As she ran, she glimpsed their heads turn toward her.

She knew they talked about her. Whispered about her. Cursing her name. Blaming *her* for the colony's troubles.

Too much to bear. Catherine needed the comfort of her mother's arms.

The Hatchetts lived in a tiny wooden house with a sloped roof. Catherine ran straight into the open doorway.

She banged into her mother's back. Martha Hatchett carried a large black kettle toward the fireplace. Some of the broth sloshed over onto the bare planks of the floor.

"Catherine!" Mistress Hatchett exclaimed angrily. "Why do you never watch what you are doing? If you are not going to be at home when you should be to help your own mother prepare the family meal, then you must—"

Her mother stopped short, studying her. "Now what have you done to yourself! Your face is a mask of dirt. And that dress! Do you have no idea of the value of things, Catherine? Do you think your poor father can afford to keep you in new clothes when times are already so hard?"

"But, Mama . . . I . . . The boys . . ."

"I don't want to hear any of it. You have caused enough trouble for one day. You have caused enough trouble for a lifetime!"

"But . . . how can you say that? I did nothing wrong."

Her mother crossed to the fireplace. She carefully hung the pot on a hook over the fire. Catherine followed her, tugging at her mother's sleeve. "Mama, please, do not turn away from me. Mama! The boys . . . at school . . ."

"What?" Mistress Hatchett's eyes narrowed. "Were you bothering Master Porter again? Your father and I have warned you time and time again not to go near—"

"But the boys, they all chanted at me, calling me names. Bad Luck Catherine. That is what they all—"

Her mother grabbed her shoulders. "Listen to me, Catherine. You *are* bad luck, and that is the shameful truth. Born under a bad moon."

"No! I—"

"Then what is this?"

Martha Hatchett roughly grasped her daughter's head in her hands. Pushed back the brown, shiny locks that covered the girl's temple. "Here. You feel this? Your birthmark, Catherine."

Catherine twisted her head, trying to pull away, but her mother held her firmly.

Catherine knew the birthmark well. She had studied it for hours, tracing it with her fingers. It almost always made her cry. She found the mark so hideous.

Catherine covered the livid red stain, shaped like a crescent moon, with one hand. The skin felt raised and puckered. So ugly.

Mistress Hatchett released her daughter's head. Tears glistened in her eyes. "Born under a bad moon," she went on miserably. "And so you will always bring bad fortune!"

"No!" Catherine cried.

She stepped back, glanced uncertainly toward the door.

"Where are you going?" her mother demanded. "You do not have permission to leave. Do you hear me, Catherine? Catherine!"

Catherine heard, but she did not stop. Did not turn

back. Her own mother called her the same names as those boys.

She ran until her mother's cries had grown dim in her ears. Soon she reached the thick, green woods surrounding the small colony. Within the dark, cool shelter of the thick trees, she felt a little better. For here there were no people. The trees would never call her names, or accuse her of spoiling the crops. The piney smell made her feel clean, even though her face was stained with tears and dirt.

After she had wandered a little farther into the woods, her feet began to direct her. Telling her to choose this trail over that. And once again she made her way to the tiny house where the old woman lived.

The old woman was known as Crazy Gwendolyn because she chose to live all by herself. Not so crazy, thought Catherine. After all the suffering Catherine had endured, the idea of living by herself—far away from the world—made a great deal of sense.

But even Catherine found Gwendolyn strange in some ways. No one knew where she came from or how she had arrived in the colony. Strange roars had been heard coming from her house late at night. People whispered that she had captured a demon and used it for her slave. But no one had ever spied it.

Catherine pulled a cluster of pine needles off a branch and chewed them as she walked. She scolded herself for thinking harshly of Gwendolyn. The old woman treated her with more kindness than anyone in the entire colony.

Catherine knew about rumors. Was it true that Catherine had brought the bad luck to the colony? No!

So why should she believe the frightening rumors about Gwendolyn?

She spotted the small cabin with its grimy gray planks up ahead. The cabin nestled among the trees, almost as if it were part of the woods.

She ran toward it. Then through the open front door.

Empty.

No clothes hung on the wooden pegs on the wall. The fireplace dark and cold. What would she do if Gwendolyn had moved away? Or died? Then there would be no one—no one in the world Catherine could turn to.

"Catherine," called a raspy voice.

She whirled around.

In the doorway stood the tall figure of Gwendolyn Parrish. As always, she held herself straight, not stooped with age. Her long silver hair curved down to her waist. Her face was creased and cracked and whiskery.

"Ah, Catherine, my poor Catherine. Have they been so cruel to you again?"

Catherine did not have to tell her what had happened. Gwendolyn already knew. She always knew.

Catherine ran to her. Gwendolyn threw her arms open wide and hugged her. Her bony arms clung to Catherine like vines.

"There, there, Catherine. You will survive these bad times, I promise you that. I know you feel as though the pain is too great, but you have my word, you will survive."

Catherine pressed closer against her, her hot tears

soaking into the woman's dress. "They . . . names . . . cursing me . . . even my mother . . ."

"I know, I know . . ."

The old woman patted her back a few times, then gently moved her away. "Come," Gwendolyn said, "I will make you some sassafras tea that will soothe your heart. But I think you have forgotten my words of advice."

"I h-have?"

"Did I not tell you to ignore what they say? No matter how cruel?" The old woman's large dark eyes shone almost red in the dark cabin, like an animal's eyes at night. "When they tease you, Catherine, imagine that they are so many bees buzzing in your ear. Simply brush them away." Gwendolyn waved her hand.

Was it the tea or was it Gwendolyn's obvious affection that worked its good magic on Catherine? Within minutes she felt as if her horrible day had been swept from her mind.

She stayed with Gwendolyn until dusk. She did not want to leave then.

"Come, Catherine," Gwendolyn said at last, walking her to the cabin door. "You must go. Your parents will be very angry if you make the family wait for its meal."

Catherine turned back twice as she headed into the dark woods. The first time she found Gwendolyn framed in the large dark doorway, her silver hair blowing in the breeze. The second time, Gwendolyn had disappeared.

The woods by night did not comfort Catherine as

they did by day. Everything she heard filled her with fear. Her footsteps crunching on fallen leaves and twigs. The hooting of owls. The drone of insects.

And then she heard a sound that made her heart pound.

Footsteps crackled behind her.

She stopped. The footsteps stopped as well.

Someone followed her.

chapter
3

Catherine turned back into the dark woods. She could see nothing but the large, dark trees. Their leaves swayed like shadowy ghosts. "Who is there?"

No answer but the caw of a bird. She backed up a few steps. And hit something hard.

A tree trunk. She started to run.

The footsteps behind her grew louder now. Something crashed through the brush. Perhaps a bear making its charge!

Gasping, Catherine ran faster. Her hand smashed against a tree. But she couldn't stop to wait for the pain to fade.

Faster, faster. And then the tip of her shoe caught a tree root.

She fell as hard as if she had been shot in the back. She tasted blood. She had cut her lip.

When she sat up, pine needles stuck to her face like cat's whiskers. She saw a pair of leather shoes.

And then another pair.

She pushed herself to her knees. Joseph and William Parker stared down at her.

Joseph's leather hat tilted back on his head, showing off his handsome face and blond hair. But right now that face glowed darkly with anger.

"Get up," he ordered.

Catherine obeyed. "W-why did you chase me? Why did you scare me so when I—"

"Be quiet," William snapped. He stood shorter than his older brother. Not quite as good-looking. His face wider and softer than Joseph's.

Usually Catherine thought him more kind-hearted than his brother. But now he sounded just as angry. Just as fierce.

"My father says our pigs are dying because of you!" William accused. "Bad Moon Catherine!"

"That is a lie!" Catherine protested. She forced herself not to cover the crescent-shaped scar on her temple.

"You are to blame for the bad crops!" William went on. "Because of you, everyone is going hungry." His face twisted with anger. "I suppose you do not feel shame. No matter. They will soon banish you from the West Hampshire Colony, Bad Moon Catherine! I heard them talking."

24

She tried to remember Gwendolyn's advice, told herself not to listen. But terror gripped her. She could not think. "Who? Who has been talking?"

"You will find out soon enough."

The brothers closed in on her, one from each side. She inched backward, but William caught her hand.

What are they planning to do to me? she wondered.

"All right, William," Joseph said sharply. "Let her go. I will take care of her. You run on home."

William stared at his brother. "But it is not safe, Joseph. Who knows what strange powers she has, what she might try. . . ."

"Do not worry," Joseph reassured him. "I will take care of her, I promise you."

The way he said the words made Catherine tremble.

"Go!" Joseph commanded his younger brother.

"Yes, Joseph," he muttered. He turned and stalked off, disappearing quickly into the dark shadows of the woods.

Catherine faced Joseph. All alone in the darkness. His eyes gleamed.

Joseph moved closer. Catherine backed away.

She felt thorns tearing at her clothes. Scratching her skin like tiny knives.

Tall thorn bushes formed a wall behind her.

Joseph reached for her.

She could not escape.

chapter
4

Joseph grabbed her face with both hands, squeezing hard. His blue eyes angrier than ever.

He kissed her full on the lips.

Shocked, Catherine did not move. She did not breathe.

But as he pulled her away from the thorn bush, she began to return his kiss. Her hands flew around his neck. She could not help herself. She felt so lonely, so hungry for affection.

He lifted her up into the air and spun her around, laughing. Then he braced her against the silver, peeling bark of a birch tree and lowered his lips to hers. This kiss longer, slower, lingering.

He smiled down at her. Gently he pulled off her white cap, letting her long brown hair flow freely down her shoulders and back. Then he reached a hand up toward her temple. She jerked her head back, frightened.

"It is all right, Catherine. Do not be afraid."

She felt his fingers gently tracing the red crescent moon of her birthmark. Then he bent down to kiss her again.

She moved her head away. "Why are you doing this? To ridicule me?"

"Because I care for you," Joseph replied kindly.

The genuine affection in his blue eyes stunned her. Joseph's father was one of the village elders. If he found out that Joseph cared about Bad Moon Catherine . . .

Catherine began to laugh. She could not stop. Frightened and excited, she turned to run home.

"Catherine!"

She stopped. Joseph stood in the darkness, staring at her.

She ran back to him, into his arms. He hugged her tight. After a moment he murmured, "I have watched you, Catherine, for a long time."

"You have?" she asked, pressing her face against his broad chest. She felt glad he could not see the amazement on her face.

He kissed the top of her head. "Oh," she uttered softly.

He moved back to arm's length. His blue eyes searched hers.

She darted forward and planted light feathery kisses over his fine features. Not missing a spot. Sure to kiss even his dimple.

"I must go," she told him. "I am so late and—"

"But you will meet me again?"

The question thrilled her.

"Yes! Yes!"

Catherine raced home. She felt as though the wind carried her. Could it be? All at once her bad luck had turned into gold. Gold hair and a dimple!

A crowd had gathered in front of the town meetinghouse. Tacked to the door was a public notice. The banns of marriage, announcing the betrothal of Joseph Parker and Catherine Hatchett.

"Who would have believed that such an unlucky girl would end up marrying such a fine young man?" murmured one of the townspeople. "Joseph is so handsome, so well respected."

"Well, it is not so surprising, really," commented another woman. "She is so pretty, as pretty as he is good-looking. And do you know she is smart as well? Why, I hear they say she is smarter than any man."

"And here we thought she brought us bad luck," muttered a third woman, shaking her head. "When actually she is the most special and gifted woman of us all."

"Catherine," her mother snapped. "Catherine! Do you have ears? Do you not hear me talking to you?"

Catherine shook her head. The daydream vanished. She stood in her house, gazing down at a bare dining table. A table she should be setting.

"Where are the mugs? Where is your father's trencher? Honestly, Catherine, is there nothing you can do right?"

"I am sorry, Mama," Catherine replied. She hurried about her task, setting out the large ceramic pitcher of hard cider they drank with every meal. Next she placed the mugs, napkins, and wooden trencher plates on the table.

But her mind drifted back . . . to Joseph. The marriage had been a fantasy, but . . .

Three weeks had passed since that first shocking kiss in the woods. Since then the woods had become Catherine and Joseph's magical hiding place. They met there almost every day.

Joseph treated her with such tenderness. Such kindness. Even so, Catherine could not shake her fear that Joseph toyed with her. Took advantage of her loneliness.

She did not want to believe that. She wanted to believe him sincere.

A bolt of lightning zigzagged through the dark sky outside the house. A crash of thunder followed at once.

The ferocious storm had raged all day, and some of the night before.

"I pray your father journeys home safely in this horrible weather," her mother murmured.

As if in response to her prayer, Adam Hatchett strode through the door. Water dripped from the wide brim of his dark hat. His face appeared pale and wet.

"Adam, you are well?" Martha Hatchett asked. She hurried to take his coat.

"I wish that I were," Catherine's father replied gravely. He stared at Catherine as he spoke.

Catherine slowly lowered the mug she held.

"This storm is the final straw, Catherine," he announced. He sounded as though he blamed her. "It has destroyed the last of our crops," he went on. "The cattle are dying in the fields. *Dying.*" Adam Hatchett's voice broke. He wiped the water from his face with his sleeve. "So much bad luck. So much *unnatural* luck. We could all starve to death this coming winter, do you realize that?

"Why were you so late coming home, father?" Catherine asked, dreading the answer.

"Some of the men needed to speak to me," he replied, glancing away.

"What is it?" Mistress Hatchett asked. Catherine could hear the worry in her mother's voice.

"Edmund Parker called a town meeting to discuss our troubles," her father said.

Edmund Parker—Joseph's father!

Adam Hatchett turned his cold eyes on Catherine. Sternly he added, "It is a meeting to discuss what to do about you."

part

2

Shadyside
1995

chapter

5

"There is nothing to discuss, Bryan," declared Mr. Robbins. "You've got to straighten out, that's all. I'm serious. This is the last time I'm going to warn you."

"I don't know how it happened," Bryan Folger replied sheepishly. He could feel his stomach churning, the way it always did when someone chewed him out. "These registers must be defective or something."

"They are not defective," Mr. Robbins said, scowling. The pudgy man bent over the cash register, trying to remove the jammed roll of white paper. "You kept pressing the *Receipt After Sale* button, Bryan. I saw you. I mean, what were you thinking about?"

"Uh . . ."

"Why can't you ever pay attention to what you're doing?"

Maybe because this job is so boring, thought Bryan. Especially compared to what I had been thinking about.

The sleek white sports car at Denny's used car lot. The car he needed to own. His girlfriend Misty was right, of course. He shouldn't care so much about an object, a thing.

But ever since he and his friend Alan stepped onto the lot and found that car, he knew he had to own it.

If only he were in that car right now, cruising through town, picking up Misty. *Hey, Misty, want to go for a ride?*

"I mean, when I hired you, you promised me you were Happy Burgers material." The manager pulled hard on the roll of paper. The paper jammed more tightly. Mr. Robbins cursed. "You said you would dedicate yourself to making our customers happy. Do you remember saying that?"

Bryan remembered. He also remembered thinking that Mr. Robbins was a sad case. Single, bald, overweight. Caring so much about a job at Happy Burgers. He remembered praying that he never ended up like Mr. Robbins.

That first day Mr. Robbins made Bryan recite the Happy Burgers motto: "Happy Burgers Means Happy Eaters." Then Mr. Robbins solemnly presented him with a Happy Burgers apron with its huge yellow smiley face splashed across the center.

"You got the job!" Mr. Robbins exclaimed with a big grin. As if Bryan had won the lottery or something.

But it's a job, Bryan reminded himself. Minimum wage, yes. But added to his other part-time work delivering flowers, this job would help him put a down payment on . . . The Car.

The front door jingled. Bryan glanced up. So did Mr. Robbins.

A middle-aged man hurried in. He shook the rain from his beige raincoat and stamped his feet.

Mr. Robbins continued in a low voice, "I just don't know if you've got the proper attitude, Bryan. I mean, if you don't want the job, just say so. I have a long list of people who would love to wear the Happy Burgers smile."

"I want the job," Bryan assured him. He'd never felt sorrier for himself. Or Mr. Robbins.

"All right," Mr. Robbins said, "I'll take care of this. You wait on our customer."

"Yes, sir."

Bryan moved to the other register as the customer walked over. Bryan plastered a big smile on his face. Mr. Robbins expected all the Happy Burgers employees to smile constantly. Normally, Bryan didn't bother about that rule. But with Mr. Robbins already furious with him, he figured he'd better be on his best behavior.

"Welcome to Happy Burgers. How can we help make your night a happy one?"

"Give me one large Happy Fries—"

Bryan pressed the button on the register's plastic-coated keypad, entering the price. "One large Happy Fries."

"And a small chocolate Happy Shake."

"And a small chocolate Happy Shake," Bryan repeated.

But before he could press the shake button, he remembered the question he needed to ask every customer before taking their order. "Is this for here or to go?"

Fast.

The image of the white car zoomed through Bryan's mind.

Then he looked down. He had pressed the cola button by mistake.

"Whoops. Mr. Robbins? I need a void."

"Oh, for pete's sake!" Mr. Robbins grumbled. He fumbled for his keys.

"You know what?" the customer said. "I'm in a kind of a big rush here. My wife and kid are in the car. The kid is screaming. We're late for a surprise party. Well, anyway, the point is—I'll pay extra. I don't care. Just give me the food."

Bryan couldn't help feeling jealous. This guy had money to throw around, and Bryan had to watch every penny. Bryan kept track of his income and expenses in a small lined notebook. "We can't do that," he explained.

"Why?"

"Because our totals won't match at the end of the day. Anyway, this will only take a sec."

The customer peered out the front of the restaurant. He shifted nervously from foot to foot.

Mr. Robbins elbowed Bryan aside. "I'll ring it up. You get the customer's food. Do you think you can do *that* right?"

Bryan's face reddened. He felt so angry he wanted to quit on the spot. But if he gave up this job, how would he ever own the Cataluna?

"What are you standing there for?" Mr. Robbins cried. "Didn't you hear the customer say he was in a hurry?"

"Yes, sir." He hurried to the shake machine. "Vanilla, right?" he asked the customer.

"Chocolate!" the man snapped.

"Right." Man, now *both* of them are on my case! Bryan thought.

He filled the shake cup to the brim and snapped on a white plastic cap. "And one large Happy Fries, coming right up."

Mr. Robbins had finished ringing up the order. Bryan crossed to the french fry bin. "Oh, no." He found only two cold fries sticking to the bottom of the silver tray. He stared into the wire fry basket. He had forgotten to add the fries! Even though Mr. Robbins had told him several times to make a new batch.

How could I have done that? I'm such a moron.

He glanced back at the customer. Then he stuck the fry basket in the grease and quickly bent down and opened the freezer. He pulled out another white bag of Happy fries. When he ripped open the bag, frozen fries scattered everywhere.

"You're not making the fries from scratch, are you?" the customer asked with a loud sigh.

"Well, I—"

Mr. Robbins stared at him.

"It will only take a second," Bryan muttered.

Mr. Robbins strode over to the counter and stared

down at the empty french fry bin. "You i-idiot!" he sputtered. "I must have told you a hundred times!"

"I'm sorry," Bryan said. To the customer he added, "It will only take a sec, I promise." He tried to dump the rest of the bag of frozen fries into the basket covered with scalding oil. Mr. Robbins blocked his way.

"Oh, forget it," the customer said. He grabbed his shake and stalked out of the restaurant.

"Sir?" Mr. Robbins called after him. "You paid for the fries! Sir? Please come back anytime and have a free Happy dinner on the house! Sir?!"

The door jangled. The man disappeared.

Mr. Robbins turned back to Bryan, his eyes cold. "That's it," Mr. Robbins declared. "That is it!"

Bryan had one hand on the fry basket, still ready to make the fries. "I don't know how I forgot, Mr. Robbins. I—"

"I'm afraid you have to leave, Bryan."

"What? Oh, no, please, Mr. Ro—"

"Please take off that Happy Burgers apron. You're through."

"Please, Mr. Robbins. Don't do that. I really need this job. I promise I'll—"

"You promise! Your promise means nothing to me. You've shown me that, Bryan." Mr. Robbins waved a pudgy finger in Bryan's face. The same thing Bryan's father did when he got mad. "You've used up all your chances."

Bryan had never been fired before. He felt close to tears. "That is so unfair!"

Mr. Robbins shut his eyes. "Go home, Bryan."

Bryan stared at him.

"I said, go home," Mr. Robbins repeated. "I'll send you your last paycheck for these last two days. Minus whatever you owe me if a repairman has to come in here and fix that register."

"No way! You can't do that!"

Mr. Robbins didn't bother to answer.

"I said no way!"

Mr. Robbins went back to work on the register as if he hadn't heard. As if Bryan didn't even exist.

Bryan felt the rage swell up in his chest.

He stared down at his hand. He still clenched the wire handle of the silver fry basket. He pulled the basket out of the hot oil.

"Mr. Robbins?"

He spoke quietly, but Mr. Robbins glanced up.

Bryan swung the basket. He let out an angry cry as the scalding hot grease flew over the manager.

Mr. Robbins clutched his face and began to howl.

chapter
6

"Noooo!" Mr. Robbins let out a high, shrill wail. He ran forward, grabbing blindly for the counter. "Help me!"

Bryan dropped the wire basket to the tiled floor.

How could he have done that? It felt as if an alien force controlled his hand.

Too late to take it back. Too late. He had scalded the man.

He lurched toward Mr. Robbins, his hands outstretched to catch him. "Mr. Robbins, I'm so sorry, I—"

"Get away from me!" Mr. Robbins shrieked.

Bryan felt the horror eat through him. He had

attacked his boss. He was going to jail. In one instant he had thrown away his entire life.

Mr. Robbins suddenly stopped screaming. He gazed down at his hands. He rubbed his cheeks. Relief spread across his wet face. "It's cold!" he breathed.

Cold. Slowly the word worked its way into Bryan's brain.

Mr. Robbins laughed. "You *fool*. You even forgot to turn on the fryer, didn't you? Didn't you?!"

Mr. Robbins ripped the Happy Burgers apron from around Bryan's neck. He grabbed Bryan by the collar and shoved him toward the door. Bryan could feel the cold french fry grease on Mr. Robbins's hands.

"Out. And stay out!" Mr. Robbins shouted as he pushed Bryan outside.

Gray sheets of rain slashed down against the black pavement of the parking lot. Head down, Bryan trudged past several parked cars until he came to his beat-up ten-speed. He spent an entire summer working a paper route to buy this bike. Now he hated it.

Bryan rode through the pouring rain. Each time he shoved down on the pedals, the word *fired* blasted through his brain.

Fired. Fired. Fired.

Bryan passed Denny's car lot. No chance he'd ever own the sleek white car now.

He allowed himself a quick glance. Yes. The Cataluna still sat in the parking lot. No one had bought it. Yet.

The rain slowed by the time he got home fifteen minutes later.

"You're home early," his mother called from the kitchen. "Everything okay?"

"Yeah, Mom," he answered, hurrying upstairs. "Just fine." His mother always worried about him. How would she feel when she found out he couldn't even hold down a part-time job at Happy Burgers?

Bryan took a shower and changed into dry clothes. Then he fed his goldfish, Joe and Montana. Pet food and pet accessories were some of the expenses he kept track of in his notebook. But he never regretted the money he spent on them.

He thought about calling Misty. But he couldn't stand the thought of telling her the news over the phone. "Hi, Misty. You know how you are always secretly looking down on me because you're rich and I'm poor? You deny it, but I know you do. Well, guess what? I got fired, so now I'm even poorer!"

No way.

The rain finally stopped. Water dripped off the trees. He hurried downstairs, past the living room where the TV blared. His father watching Monday Night Football. Bryan called that he had to go back out again. He banged out the front door before his mother could answer.

Misty lived in a big house in the North Hills section of Shadyside. A twenty-minute bike ride. I have as much right to be here as anyone else, Bryan told himself as he pedaled down the wide tree-lined streets. But he felt like an intruder in this neighborhood of big houses and well-kept lawns.

Bryan leaned his bike up against the big maple next

to Misty's walkway and headed for the porch. He had to ring the doorbell several times before he heard footsteps clumping down the carpeted front steps. He watched through the door's lacy curtains as his girl-friend trotted down the steps toward him.

Misty had blond hair that she wore short. The haircut made her pretty green eyes appear even larger. She bent down so that she could see who stood on the porch. She gave Bryan a big smile and a wave.

She won't be smiling for long, he thought.

"Hi, Bry!" She kissed him on the cheek. "Come in," she urged. "I'm on long distance with my cousin."

He followed her up the plush carpeting, past the framed oil paintings. Original Chagalls, Misty once told him. He didn't know anything about art. But these paintings must have cost big.

Bryan felt glad that he didn't run into Misty's father. He ran DigiComm, a big software company. He'd always been nice to Bryan. But Bryan couldn't help thinking that Mr. Clark looked down on him for being poor.

Bryan followed Misty into her room. She waved for him to sit anywhere. Then she flopped down on her canopied bed and picked up her cordless phone. "Sorry," she said, "Bry just came over. What?" She laughed. "Okay, I will." She smiled at him. "Annette says I should give you a big kiss for her."

"Sounds good," he replied. He forced a grin. He thought he should say something witty, but he couldn't think of anything. Especially not tonight.

He sat at her desk. On top he found a bag with a

stack of new CDs. He couldn't help noticing the receipt stapled to the bag: $107.39. Wow. What would it be like to spend that kind of money?

As soon as Misty hung up, he planned to tell her about getting fired. Bryan realized he had something else to explain to her. His stomach clenched.

"Sorrrry," Misty told him when she hung up. Then she sat up and grinned at him. "Hey, I thought you were working tonight."

"Yeah," he answered. Somehow he couldn't bring himself to say the words "I was fired." Not yet.

"You okay? You seem a little . . . something."

"Yeah, I guess I am. Uh, I lost my job tonight."

"At the flower shop?"

"No, at Happy Burgers."

"Oh. Well, that's good news, right? I mean, I hated the idea of you working at that place."

"It's not good news, Misty. It's not good news at all. I needed that job."

She frowned. "Sorry. So what happened?"

He thought about lying. *Oh, I don't know. They changed their schedule around and so they had to let a couple of people go. And so since I was pretty new there and all . . .*

But he'd never lied to Misty. Don't start now, Bryan told himself. She's the best thing in your life.

"I messed up. My mind kept wandering to other things, I guess. Like you."

"Well," she said, "in that case, I'm even more glad you got fired."

He winced. Fired. That sounded awful.

"There's more," he told her. "When Mr. Robbins fired me, I—I really lost my temper."

How could he have attacked Mr. Robbins? The thought of losing the Cataluna had turned him into some kind of *psycho!*

She got off the bed and leaned against her desk. "Oh, Bry," she said softly. "You're too sensitive, you know that? I'm serious. You're always apologizing to me for something you said when I've already forgotten all about it. You're allowed to get mad, you know."

She smiled at him. He gave her a weak grin. Then she bent down and kissed him on the mouth. Bryan wasn't so crazy or depressed that he couldn't still enjoy the kiss. Kissing Misty felt like a ref calling Time Out in a game. No matter how bad things were going, a kiss from her stopped everything.

After a moment she straightened and glanced self-consciously at her open door. She hurried over and swung it shut.

For the millionth time, he asked himself the question: Did Misty really like him?

Yes. Same answer as always. But Bryan never quite believed it. Bryan and Misty. They just didn't belong together.

All last spring he kept telling his best friend Alan Brown about Misty. Misty's so cool. Misty's so beautiful. Misty's so friendly. Finally Alan said he couldn't take it anymore. He made Bryan go over to Misty in the cafeteria line and ask if he could have lunch with her. His heart pounded, but he did it.

More amazing, she answered, "Sure."

During lunch he found her easy to talk to. Something about her made it easy for him to tell her what he felt. About halfway through lunch he blurted out that he thought she was the prettiest girl in the school. He admitted that he couldn't believe she had agreed to have lunch with him. She laughed and told him she'd go on a date with him, too, if he wanted.

On their first date he opened up even more, telling her stuff about his dreams and goals. Things he hadn't told anyone. Not even Alan.

"You know what?" she asked, tapping his chest with her finger. "You have a good heart, Bryan Folger." He kissed her for the first time.

She'd probably never kiss him again after she heard what he'd done. "There's more," he went on with a sigh. He fingered the plastic bag of CDs on Misty's desk. He wished he could crawl inside it. "Mr. Robbins kept riding me and riding me. You know how he's always on my case? And—I don't know—I lost it. I threw the french fry grease at him."

It felt good to tell Misty. Then he noticed the shocked expression on her face.

"He's okay," Bryan added quickly. "The oil was cold."

"Oh, you had me scared for a second. Still . . . Bry!"

"I know. I don't know what's wrong with me. It's—" He glanced at her shyly. "It's that car."

"Bryan," she scolded, "you're making yourself nuts with that thing. I'm serious. I'm starting to get jealous, you talk about that car so much."

"Sorry."

Misty wrinkled her nose at him. "Oh, hey, listen to this new CD I got." She knelt down in front of her CD player, dropped in the shiny disk, then pushed the drawer back into the deck, and pressed Play.

"Smashing Pumpkins!" he said. He loved that group.

Misty nodded. She swayed to the music. She beckoned him toward her as she started to dance.

"I can't wait for Saturday night, can you?" she said over the music.

They had decided on dinner at La Traviata, Misty's favorite Italian restaurant at the mall. Then out to the local dance club. With a cover charge of fifteen dollars each. Plus soda at the bar. And the fee for parking Misty's Ford Taurus.

"Misty," he started. He stepped away from her. Turned off the CD player.

"What? Don't turn that off. Bry!"

"Hold it a sec. I've got more bad news. Now that I lost this job, I don't think I can afford to take you dancing Saturday night. Mr. Robbins might not even give me my last paycheck."

"Oh." Misty forced a smile. "Don't worry about it, Bry. We'll stay home and rent a movie." She gave him a wink. "A much better date."

But Bryan knew she felt disappointed. Disappointed in him. She probably wanted to offer to treat him. But he'd told her over and over that he wouldn't go anywhere if he couldn't pay his own way.

He couldn't shake the bad feeling. When he left an hour later, he felt even lower than when he'd arrived.

He rode up the hill to Alan's house. The bright spotlights over the garage were on, and Bryan could hear voices laughing and shouting. He heard a basketball banging off the backboard.

Bryan rode up to the base of the driveway, leaning the bike to his left so he could rest one foot on the curb. He saw Alan shooting baskets with his younger brother. Alan dropped a layup. Swish!

"I win!" Alan yelled. He loped down the drive.

"Hey," Alan said.

"Misty broke up with me," Bryan announced.

"No way!" Alan exclaimed. He sounded shocked.

"Way."

Alan appeared so sorry for him. "I'm kidding," Bryan admitted. "But she will break up with me. I can tell."

"That's what you always say. Do the words *think positive* mean anything to you?"

"I lost my dictionary."

Alan grunted. He pulled at the bangs of his dirty blond hair. Alan liked to hide the acne on his forehead.

"I'm serious," Bryan insisted. "She's going to break up with me soon." He told Alan about getting fired, throwing the grease, canceling his date.

"Hey, Alan!" his brother called. "How about double or nothing?"

"You already lost double or nothing, fool!" Alan shouted back. He turned back to Bryan. "For the hundred zillionth time, Bryan, she's not going to break up with you. Why can't you accept the fact that you have great luck. I'm serious."

"Right. Me lucky. That is such a laugh."

"You're lucky to have Misty," Alan replied. Bryan felt bad. In two years Alan had only gone out on five dates. The only girl he didn't freeze up around was Misty, because he'd gotten to know her through Bryan.

Alan cuffed his shoulder. "Ditch the bike. My little Hyundai's in the shop again, if you can believe it. We'll take Mom's car."

"Where are we going?" Bryan asked after they climbed into the car.

Sometimes Alan's little outings scared Bryan. Alan had a wild streak. But if Alan got in any kind of trouble, his father would bail him out. Hire a fancy lawer.

Bryan's father would probably let him rot in jail. Teach him a lesson.

"Where are we going?" Bryan asked again.

Alan turned a corner and Bryan knew the answer. Denny's car lot.

Ten minutes later they stood in front of the Cataluna. The car had a beautiful finish, like a freshly poured glass of milk. Rainwater dotted the hood. Bryan wiped away some of the water with his sleeve. Then he knelt down in front of the car's silver grille, tracing the letters there—*Cataluna*.

"Alan?"

"What?"

"Do you think it's possible to fall in love with a car?"

Alan snorted. "Sure. Just don't try to make out with it."

"I'm serious. Misty told me she felt jealous of the Cataluna. And the crazy thing is, in way she's right. She *should* be jealous, man."

"It's a cool car," Alan agreed.

"Yeah. So what am I going to do? I mean, this car isn't going to sit here forever. Someone will snap it up. And now that I lost my job, I won't have the down payment for months."

"Hey, I know!" Alan said softly. "Why don't we steal it?"

chapter
7

"Right now?" Bryan asked.

"Why not?"

Bryan stared at Alan. "I know how to jump-start a car," Bryan told him. "My dad taught me."

"Go for it."

"Really?" Bryan asked.

"Let's do it."

Bryan gazed at the car. He felt as if the Cataluna understood them. Dared him to take it. Amazing thought. The Cataluna could be his. Right now.

"Whoa. It's a crazy idea," Bryan declared. "Remember what happened to those two guys who stole a car off this lot a few weeks ago? They bailed out and a truck ran over them. I don't want to end up as roadkill."

"Forget about it, then. I wasn't serious." Alan laughed.

Bryan reddened. "Me, neither," he lied. "I was just kidding around."

"For sure."

"I was! Anyway, it's easy for you to say let's do it. You're rich. Your parents could buy you *ten* Catalunas."

They both stared at the car. The sleek curves. "I'm telling you," Bryan said in a hushed voice, "this is the prettiest thing I've ever seen."

"After Misty Clark, you mean," Alan teased him.

Bryan smiled. "I don't know about that."

They both laughed. I'll find a way to get this car, Bryan thought. I know I will.

"Hi, Bry."

"Oh, hi."

"Not that I'm keeping count, but this is the sixth time I've had to call you first," Misty told him.

"Really?"

"You okay? You sound in a rush or something."

"Sorry. It's just—"

"Just what?"

He couldn't tell her. "Just nothing."

"Oh. So, anyway, you want to come over and study together?"

Her tone made it clear they wouldn't be spending all their time doing homework. Bryan wanted to see Misty. But . . .

"Uh, Misty, I'm sorry, but I can't right now."

Misty didn't answer.

Great. I've disappointed her again, Bryan thought. "I was headed out the door," he explained. He started to tell her his plan. But something stopped him. "I'm on my way to the flower store to make some deliveries," he lied.

"Bryan," she said, "you don't have to give excuses. Not to me. When you want to see me, I want to see you. It's that simple."

Misty really did care about him. Unreal. "How about I come over in like a couple of hours?" he asked a little hoarsely. "Or maybe a couple of minutes?"

"Great."

She sounded less hurt now that she knew he had to work.

Wow, Bryan thought as he hung up. That story about the flower shop is probably the first lie I ever told her. And it had been so easy. She felt better, too. Maybe he should rethink this whole honesty business.

Bryan parked and locked his bike on Laurel Avenue, a couple of blocks away from the used car lot. If the salesmen saw him ride in on his old bike, they'd never take him seriously.

He hurried over to the lot, heading straight for the Cataluna. He glanced back and forth. No one around. "Hi," he told the car. He patted the smooth curve of the hood.

Bright sunlight reflected off the windshield like a burst of fire. Bryan turned toward the glass-walled main office. He cupped a hand over his eyes to block out the glare. Why isn't anyone coming over? He made his way across the lot to the office.

A broad-shouldered man with dark shiny hair stopped talking as Bryan approached.

The other salesman, an older man, stared at Bryan. "What's up?"

"Uh, I'm . . . interested . . ." He forgot what he had planned to say. He started again. "I wanted to take one of the cars for a test-drive."

"Lou," the older salesman said, "you've got a customer."

"You got a license?" the dark-haired salesman asked.

"Uh, yes. Sure." Bryan fumbled in his pocket for his wallet. It seemed to stick to his jeans. He found the license and handed it to the salesman. Misty, Alan, and Bryan all passed their test on the same day. Only Bryan didn't have a car yet.

The young salesman handed him back the card. He's going to tell me to get lost, Bryan thought. "What kind of car were you interested in?" the salesman asked.

"Oh, I'm only interested in one car. The white sports car. The Cataluna."

The salesman whistled. "You got taste, kid. That's a beautiful car. You hear that, Jack? He wants to test-drive the Cataluna."

"Great car," the older salesman agreed.

"I love it," gushed Bryan.

The salesman eyed him. "The Cataluna is a lot of money. But we can work out the financing. You'll need to put down a thousand dollars."

Might as well be a million, Bryan thought glumly.

I'm not fooling this guy, either. He knows I don't have a dime.

A fantasy played through Bryan's mind. He pictured himself coming back tomorrow and buying the Cataluna from this same salesman. Paying in cash. And throwing in a whopping tip. "Keep the change," he'd say with a wink. Then he'd smile at the other salesman, the older guy. "Bet you wish *you* waited on me the other day. This tip would have been yours."

"A thousand down," Bryan replied, trying to sound matter-of-fact.

"You're still interested?"

"Uh-huh. Well, I mean, I don't have the whole amount right now, but I'm working on it," Bryan explained. "I'm planning to buy the car very soon."

The salesman hardly listened. "Great," he said with a sigh. He grabbed a key from his desk.

Bryan couldn't believe it. "So I can drive it?"

"Why not? It's not like I've got so much else to do."

Yes! thought Bryan, amazed. I'm going to drive the car!

Bryan hurried across the lot to the Cataluna. The salesman opened the door for him. "Hop in," he instructed.

Bryan settled into the plush red leather seat. I must be dreaming, he thought. And I never want to wake up.

The salesman climbed in the passenger side. "You okay?" he asked. "You're not going to faint on me or anything, are you?"

"I'm fine," Bryan answered quickly.

The salesman handed Bryan the ignition key. It glistened. Mother-of-pearl circled the top. Bryan held his breath as he pumped the gas once, then started the engine. The engine barely made a sound. Without the little lights glowing in the silver dashboard, he wouldn't have been sure the motor turned over.

Bryan guided the car off the lot.

"Turn right," the salesman instructed him. "We'll go down Laurel Avenue where there isn't much traffic."

The car handled beautifully. Bryan barely had to touch the wheel.

They passed Bryan's bike. It had never appeared so old and babyish to him.

Bryan slipped into another fantasy. He and Misty driving back from the prom and—

"Hi, Bryan."

The female voice startled him out of his daydream. He glanced over at the salesman. "Did you hear that?"

"Hear what?"

Bryan stared down at the radio.

Off.

"Hi, Bryan. You and I are going to have fun together."

He checked the rearview mirror.

Nothing.

"What are you searching for, Bryan?"

He turned around to study the red leather seat behind.

Empty.

He heard the girl laughing.

"Watch out!" the salesman shouted.

Bryan turned around. "Hey—I can't stop!"

"**N**ooo!"

Bryan let out a sharp cry as he slammed forward. The seatbelt dug into his chest.

He heard the crunch of metal.

Saw bright sparks fly all around.

His head snapped back hard. Pain shot down his neck. Were the sparks inside his head?

What happened?

Bryan shook his head hard. He stared groggily through the windshield.

And saw that he had smashed the car into a lamppost.

For a long while the salesman sat in stunned silence.

Then he started shouting. Calling Bryan worse names than anything Mr. Robbins ever had.

Bryan backed the car off the curb. Turned off the motor. He jumped out of the car and ran to inspect the damage. The salesman followed him.

Bryan gasped in surprise. Only a few scratches on the Cataluna's silver fender. When Bryan rubbed some spit on them, they disappeared. "The car is totally fine," Bryan uttered.

He couldn't resist a big smile. He felt so relieved. He would have wanted to die himself if he wrecked the Cataluna.

The salesman glared at him. Without another word he strode to the driver's side and got in.

"Hey, wait!" Bryan cried.

"Come back when you learn how to drive, kid!" the salesman muttered. He slammed the door. Then he pulled back out on the road and roared away.

Bryan stood stranded on the side of the road. Staring after the Cataluna. Beautiful. Amazing.

It disappeared from sight.

I need that car.

Bryan remembered the strange voice.

"You and I are going to have fun together."

I'll do anything to get the Cataluna, Bryan thought. Anything.

Bryan parked the small white minivan, leaving the engine running. He walked around and opened the double doors in back. He checked his delivery list. Sanderson, 119 Bethune Street. He found the bouquet with the matching label and started up the walk.

Two weeks had gone by, and he still hadn't found a second job to replace Happy Burgers. And his manager at the flower shop, Mr. Gunther, wouldn't add any extra hours to his delivery schedule.

Time is running out, he told himself as he rang the front bell. He wasn't the only one with eyes in his head. Anyone would want the Cataluna.

No answer at the Sanderson house. Terrific. That meant two things. Bryan would have to bring the flowers back to the store. And a different delivery boy would get the tip.

He rang again. Then he knocked. The door opened an inch. He gave it a nudge.

"Mrs. Sanderson? Flower delivery here. You have a nice bouquet."

He stuck his head inside, tried calling again. "Fancy stuff," Bryan muttered. The chrome and leather living room furniture reminded him of the things Misty and Alan had in their houses. He called one more time. No answer. Might as well leave the flowers, he thought.

He set the bouquet on the end table near the door. He turned to go.

Then he noticed the wallet. A woman's wallet. Large, thick, with a metal clasp. It lay on the glass coffee table in the living room.

"Hello?" he called again. "Mrs. Sanderson? Delivery."

He heard the deep ticking of a clock. Nothing else.

He glanced at the wallet again. Don't even think about it, he ordered himself.

But he started across the thick Oriental carpet toward the the table. And the wallet.

He stared down at the wallet. Afraid to touch it. Then he realized something that made him start to sweat.

He should have carried the flowers with him. That way, if someone walked in, he'd have an excuse for standing all the way over here, instead of by the door.

Get out of here! he silently ordered himself.

Wait, Bryan thought. I deserve a tip at least. He opened the wallet. Pulled out crisp bills.

All hundreds.

Bryan stuffed two hundreds into the front pocket of his jeans. He couldn't get the other bills back in the wallet. His hands were shaking too hard.

He crumpled the bills and shoved them inside as best he could.

He turned to leave, trembling all over, moving so quickly that he banged his knee on the glass edge of the table.

"Hey—is someone in there?" a woman called.

chapter

9

*P*anic stabbed his chest. Made him gasp.

Bryan lurched toward the front door. He caught a glimpse of a woman marching down the hallway. Right toward him.

Only one place to hide. The front coat closet.

He ducked inside, pulling the door partly closed behind him. He could smell mothballs. He wanted to press back into the row of coats, but the hangers might jangle.

He heard the woman walking around the living room.

Please don't look in the closet! he prayed. *Please don't look in here! I promise I will never ever do this again if you please don't look in the—*

The footsteps *click-clacked* against the wooden floor.

Coming toward Bryan.

They stopped outside the closet door.

Bryan's heart stopped, too.

Then he heard a rustle of cellophane. "Oh!" the woman exclaimed. "A delivery." More rustling. "Oh, that's nice. He remembered."

The footsteps clicked away. Bryan forced himself to count to ten before opening the closet door and bolting from the house. Outside, he raced down the sidewalk to his van.

Stupid, stupid, stupid, he cursed himself. Ten times as dumb as throwing that grease at Mr. Robbins. A hundred times!

At his next delivery the customer stared at him strangely. Bryan realized perspiration had run down his face and soaked his shirt.

As he returned to the florist shop, he finally started to calm down. Then he remembered the money. He had been so scared, he'd almost forgotten about it.

He pulled over to the side of the road and parked. Then he pulled out the two bills. Admired the crisp new hundreds. He didn't even know who was on a hundred dollar bill. He read the fine print. Benjamin Franklin. Hello, Ben. Nice to meet you.

He added the money to the soiled five-dollar bill in his own wallet.

That wasn't so hard, he told himself. And I'm two hundred dollars richer!

He gripped the wheel. A few hundred dollars more and he could make the down payment on the car.

And now he knew how to get that money.

Steal it.

So easy.

What could go wrong?

part

3

West Hampshire Colony
1698

chapter

10

"*I* think we all know the purpose of this meeting," Edmund Parker announced. He clasped his hands together in front of him, as if this were a Sunday prayer meeting. "For some time now our colony has suffered at the hands of evil forces. I think we all know what—or should I say who—is responsible.

"Still, we must be mindful of what we do here tonight. Do I need to remind anyone of the serious accusation we are making against Catherine Hatchett?"

Silence filled the meeting hall. Hidden in the shadowy corner by the front door, Catherine watched with horror. There sat all the elders of the town, their faces stony. No one leaped to his feet. No one shouted out a protest in her defense.

Not even her parents.

Her mother and father huddled together by themselves on one of the long wooden benches. Catherine studied their faces. They would defend her, of course. But could they persuade the whole colony of her innocence? Could two people stand up against this whole mob?

The testimonies began. "In the spring that my troubles started," said Luther Grady, nervously rubbing a finger along his bony jaw, "I found Catherine in my yard playing with our pony, Nellie. I remember I gave a terrible shudder when I spied the girl there. I think in my heart I knew that I'd been cursed. Only two weeks after that Nellie took sick and died. She died a horrible death, too, all bloated and moaning."

Angry murmurs rose from the townspeople gathered in the hall. The stories went on and on.

Catherine wanted to run, but she couldn't. She needed to hear.

One man blamed the failure of his crops on Catherine. One woman claimed that her bread hadn't risen the day Catherine gave her a strange look in the town square.

At last Edmund Parker took the floor once again. He stared right at Catherine's parents. "Everyone has spoken, I believe," Edmund Parker called. "And now the time has come to hear from the Hatchetts themselves. Adam, you have heard the sentiments of the colony here tonight. But you must speak your heart and your whole heart, unafraid of our disapproval, unminding of what we have said."

Adam Hatchett appeared deathly pale. He cleared his throat several times. When he spoke, Catherine could barely make out the words. "My wife will speak for both of us on this matter," he said quietly.

Catherine's heart pounded. Her mother stood, smoothing out the folds of her gray cloak.

Catherine began to cry silently.

Through the years, her mother had often been impatient with her, even angry. But she loved her still, Catherine knew. Her mother would stop this madness. She would never let any harm come to her daughter.

"I have listened to all your stories," Catherine's mother began, "and each story has been like a stake driven into my heart."

Catherine's tears flowed more freely.

"It hurts to hear a loved one talked about this way. Truly, I never like to complain of my burdens. But the pain of this is so terrible you could never imagine it. I know that I could not have imagined it before this day."

Yes, yes! thought Catherine.

"But—" Martha Hatchett paused.

That one word—*but*—turned Catherine's blood to ice.

"But," her mother continued sadly, "Adam and I know—have known for some time—that something is terribly wrong with Catherine. We have tried to blind ourselves to the truth. But now . . ."

Martha Hatchett lifted a hand, let it fall. "There is no other choice. I understand that now. We must drive the bad luck from our colony."

The crowd erupted in bloodthirsty cheers.

Catherine could not move. Could not breathe.

I did not hear right, she told herself. Could not have! Could not have!

Her father leaped to his feet. "She is not our child!" he called hoarsely.

Catherine felt as though her head had split down the middle. Not their child? What was he saying?

Several people gasped. A few rose to their feet.

"What does he mean?"

"He is lying!"

"No!" Adam Hatchett cried. "I tell the truth, at last. Our own child died at birth. We found Catherine on our doorstep."

That is a lie! Catherine silently prayed. That is a lie!

"Please forgive us," begged Adam Hatchett. "We had hoped and prayed for a family for so long. Then our baby——"

He hung his head, weeping. He could not go on.

Martha Hatchett spoke for him, continuing the confession. "And so we took Catherine in, and we never said a word."

More cries from the villagers.

"A grave sin," admitted Mistress Hatchett. "But how could we know? How could we know she was a child of evil!"

When the meeting quieted back down at last, her mother and father each told stories about the horrors of raising Catherine.

Catherine no longer heard them. The room was spinning. Her own parents! Lying. Betraying her. Denying her birth. No!

She pressed herself against the wall, but there was nowhere to go. Catherine started for the door. Tripped.

Heads turned.

She ran.

She jumped off the wooden porch and started across the lawn. Then she stopped again, gasping for air as if she had been running for miles. She glanced left, right.

Which way? Where could she go?

Catherine whirled and faced the doorway to the meeting house. She expected the townspeople to come pouring out like a swarm of angry hornets leaving the hive.

No one came.

Maybe no one had seen her after all.

An idea had formed in her mind. A place she could turn to for refuge. She raced toward the house with the dying cabbage patch in back.

Joseph Parker always warned her not to come to his house. It's not safe, he told her. They could meet only in the woods.

But now nowhere in the colony was safe for Catherine. And she had only one friend left. She had to find him right away.

Joseph. Joseph loved her. Joseph would protect her. She would not have to face this evil, this horror, alone.

She raced past the Parkers' fenced-in garden and around to the front. Banged in through the front door.

And gasped.

chapter

11

Joseph sat by the fireplace, his strong arms wrapped around a pretty redheaded girl. The girl had a spray of freckles across her apple cheeks. When Catherine burst into the room, both Joseph and the girl turned and stared at her in shock.

Joseph with another girl. That meant he did not love her. Her last dream, her last hope, crumbled before her eyes.

But she did not have time. Not for jealousy. Not to feel her heart break. Even though the hurt and anger seared through her like fire.

Joseph!" she cried. "You—you must help me! The whole town, the meeting, your father—they're going to banish me!"

Joseph stared at her blankly. "Yes, Catherine, so they are. And what do you expect me to do about it? Did you want me to ride you out of town myself?" He smiled at the girl and both of them started laughing.

Please, no, she thought. No.

"Joseph, I—" She couldn't go on. Hot tears stung her cheeks.

"It is your own fault," she heard the girl say nastily. "You've brought this down on yourself."

Catherine felt the rage surging inside her. She wanted to claw at the girl's eyes.

But she turned back to Joseph. "Joseph, there is no time to waste. Please! I heard them, with my own ears. If I ever meant anything to you—"

Joseph stood swiftly. "And what could a witch like you mean to me, eh, Catherine? What vile lies are you spinning now? How dare you come into a respectable home and—"

Catherine backed away. She stumbled out the door.

She heard more laughter from inside the cottage.

Then she turned and fled.

Rage made her run faster than she had ever run in her life. Crazy! she silently shouted at herself. Crazy to trust a boy like Joseph.

No. She could turn to only one person. The one true friend who had stood by her all these years. Gwendolyn. She ran into the dark woods, ran until she reached the old woman's cabin.

She found Gwendolyn rocking by the fire. The old

woman's eyes glittered with anger. Catherine gasped for breath. She could not speak. But Gwendolyn knew everything.

Gwendolyn kept rocking, her eyes locked on Catherine's. "The town has reached its decision?"

Catherine nodded, not even pausing to wonder how the news had reached Gwendolyn so fast.

"They have ruled that you are to blame?"

"Y-yes."

Gwendolyn appeared calm. Catherine tried to take some comfort in that.

"And here I have tried to live in peace with these people for so long. These fools believe you have caused their bad luck?" the old woman demanded harshly. "It is time to show them some *real* bad luck."

Gwendolyn stood slowly. She pulled back her lips and let out a long animal hiss.

Catherine trembled. Was Gwendolyn truly crazy?

Catherine wanted to run. But her legs would not cooperate.

Gwendolyn's whiskery face began to darken. The whiskers grew longer.

It is so dark in this cabin, Catherine thought. My eyes are tricking me.

Then Gwendolyn uttered a longer hiss. A hiss of pain.

Needle-sharp claws popped out of her outstretched fingertips.

Gwendolyn's long silver hair whirled around her body as if it had come alive. Wherever it touched her skin, the skin turned black. And furry.

Moments later tall old Gwendolyn Parrish no longer stood before Catherine. In her place stood a black cat.

The old cat stretched, arching its back. Then the cat cried, "Come, Catherine, you can do it, too! You are a shape-shifter! You are my daughter."

chapter
12

The old cat's yellow eyes locked on hers.

"I—I don't believe—" Catherine stammered.

"Believe," the cat urged her.

Catherine remembered her father's cry in the town meeting. *She is not our child!* Was it possible?

"Your daughter?" she murmured. "I do not understand—"

"I had no husband, Catherine. Please. Understand. I did not fear the shame for myself. But they would have teased you and tortured you. I could not bear the thought of that. . . ."

Gwendolyn's voice trailed off. Catherine knew what Gwendolyn was thinking. Catherine had been an outcast all the same. She had not escaped her fate.

"And so?" Catherine prompted.

"And so, one night, during a storm, I sneaked into the village. I bundled you up. And I left you on the doorstep of a respectable and childless couple. No one, not even the Hatchetts, ever knew where you came from."

All these years of misery, thought Catherine, all these years of not fitting in. As dazed and thunderstruck as she felt, Catherine knew in her heart that Gwendolyn told her the truth. She had never belonged in the Hatchett house. Never.

"You were born under the same evil moon as I was," Gwendolyn continued in her raspy purr.

Catherine suddenly felt dizzy. She braced herself with one hand against the rough wooden wall.

"At first the Hatchetts seemed overjoyed with their good luck. As painful as it was for me, I felt sure I had made the right decision," Gwendolyn explained. "But then the troubles started. Well, Catherine, you know the rest of the story only too well. You know all the bad luck that has struck the colony."

Catherine nodded.

The cat's eyes glinted. "At last we are reunited. But we must hurry. Change, Catherine. Now."

"I cannot." Catherine collapsed to the floor. Her eyes rolled back in her head.

The cat licked her cheek with its rough tongue, bringing her back to consciousness. Purring its harsh voice in her ear. "Change, Catherine. Change!"

I'm dreaming, Catherine thought, turning away.

Her mind raced over her hundreds of visits to

Gwendolyn's cabin. In one blinding flash Catherine realized she had always belonged with Gwendolyn.

The moment this thought crossed her mind, she felt a horrible pain. Her face contorted.

She had never felt pain so intense. I am dying, she thought.

She raised her hands to her face. The pain shot through her. She had scratched herself. Deep scratches.

She gave a cry that sounded more like a hiss. She stared down at her hands in amazement. Sharp curved claws stuck out of each finger.

"Change! Change!"

Intense pain, like a hot branding iron sizzling her flesh, made Catherine arch her back and howl. She heard her bones bending, cracking. She let out another animal cry. And another.

She caught glimpses of herself. Herself that was no longer herself. Shiny lustrous hair spreading all over her body. The hair turned coal black as if it had been charred in a fire.

"Yes, yes, that is right, Catherine . . ."

In a minute more she had changed completely. She was a cat. Black like her mother, only younger, smaller. Her coat shiny black without a touch of silver.

Gwendolyn hurried to the front door. Catherine followed. They padded through the woods together. It felt so strange to be running on four feet. Yet natural at the same time.

They reached a clearing in the dark woods.

Gwendolyn paused, her tail bristling. Then she threw back her head and yowled, showing her fangs.

Catherine gazed upward through a break in the trees. Hanging high above them shone a crescent moon. She opened her mouth, letting her own cat's yowl mingle with her mother's.

Gwendolyn led the way. Back into the town. Catherine felt afraid. But she followed.

They darted along the back of the meetinghouse, staying in the shadows. Was the meeting still going on?

Her hearing much keener than before, Catherine knew that the meeting hall stood empty. They were all out searching for her, no doubt.

But Catherine Hatchett had disappeared. They would never find her now.

Gwendolyn padded on, through the narrow lane between the two buildings.

All at once Catherine knew their destination.

Joseph's house.

Up ahead, Gwendolyn rubbed her cheek again and again against the side of the Parker house. Marking her territory.

They turned the corner. The front door stood slightly ajar.

Catherine sniffed the air. She caught a familiar scent. Her sense of smell must have grown more powerful as well. She could recognize Joseph's presence all the way from here.

"Use your instinct, Catherine!" purred her mother. "Take your revenge!"

The door stood open only a few inches. Catherine

stared into the dark space. She felt frightened. But she trotted forward, pushing through the opening.

Her sharp eyes adjusted quickly to the dimness inside the cabin. Joseph sat in the large high-backed wooden chair by the wall. His hat off, his legs crossed. He laughed at something. As he had laughed at her.

At the sight of him, all fear left Catherine, replaced by hate. She raced forward.

Then sprang.

He did not turn until the moment she leaped off the floor. His face, full of shock and fear, presented her with a clear target.

Yowling furiously, Catherine raked her claws across Joseph's face. The deep gouges filled with blood. The blood flowed in rivulets, down his cheeks.

She clawed him again.

This time she aimed higher.

His eyes.

Joseph shrieked. He raised his hands to protect himself.

Too late.

His left eyeball popped like a bubble.

Catherine slashed her claws across his right eye.

Again and again.

Catherine did not quit until both eyeballs lay on the floor at her feet.

chapter

13

Joseph's hoarse screams rattled the beams of the cottage.

What a wonderful sound! Catherine thought.

She stared up at his empty eye sockets. Those beautiful blue eyes were no more. Never again would they twinkle as they tricked another girl!

Joseph collapsed in a heap.

She dropped back down to the floor. Then she sat on her haunches and daintily licked his blood off her paws. The blood tasted almost as delicious as her triumph.

Something moved to her left.

She froze, her black paw still at her mouth.

In a flash she remembered how Joseph had been

laughing when she came in. How his head had been turned to his left.

There was someone else in the room.

Then she spotted him.

Joseph's brother William.

The boy's chest heaved in terror.

William moved forward cautiously.

Catherine's own heart beat faster.

What would he do?

William watched her closely, taking one step at a time. He moved closer. Did he think she would run? He stood between her and the door.

Between her and freedom.

Use your instincts, Gwendolyn had said.

Catherine let out a furious hiss. She made her shiny black hair stand on end.

William shrank back.

It worked!

What a coward, she scoffed.

Then William dived forward—and grabbed her around the throat with both hands.

chapter

14

With a frantic cry William squeezed Catherine's throat, choking off her breath.

He twisted her head. Tried to break her neck.

She pulled back with all her might. Tried to work her head out of his grasp.

His hands slipped. She sank her white fangs deep into the meat of William's palm.

"Aaiiiee!" he cried out—and hurled her to the floor.

She lay there for a moment. Too dazed to move. Then, pulling herself up, Catherine raced out of the house. Into the night.

Gwendolyn? Where are you?

Catherine could not find Gwendolyn anywhere. She

heard William running after her. He had hurt her. Hurt her badly. She gasped for breath.

She dragged herself around the corner of the house. Slinked through the slats in the fence of the garden. She pulled herself a few yards along the cold hard soil, then stopped.

She heard William's footsteps. Very close.

He is going to catch me.

I am going to die.

Then she remembered her mother's words.

You are a shape-shifter, too!

Yes! She had changed from a girl to a cat. Perhaps she could also change from cat to girl.

A moment later William limped around the side of the house. He cradled his bleeding hand against his body.

Catherine stood against the wall, shaking out her long brown hair. She saw William's eyes go wide with amazement.

"Catherine!" he gasped. "Did you see a black cat running? It clawed—It clawed—" William broke off.

Catherine shook her head. "Stay away from black cats, William," she warned coyly. "Black cats mean bad luck."

She gave him a smile, then hurried off into the darkness.

Lucky for me the moon is not full, thought Catherine, trying to catch her breath. If there had been a little more light, William might have noticed the red marks his fingers had left on my neck.

She made her way through the empty town in triumph. She had taken her revenge on Joseph. More than that. She had found her true nature. Her true home. The colony that had tortured her and scared her for so long would hold no power over her anymore.

She turned toward her parents'—her *foster* parents'—house to gather her belongings. The small house lay covered in darkness. Deserted.

As she walked up the wooden steps to the front door, it opened. Adam Hatchett blocked her way. She saw the musket in his hands.

He raised the musket, pointing it at her chest.

"The bad luck must die," he said.

Then he pulled the trigger.

part

4

Shadyside
1995

chapter

___

15

"Nice? Is that all you can say? It's *nice?*"

"Bryan," Misty complained, "I already told you it's a great-looking car. Give me a break, okay? I mean, what do you want me to do? Kiss it?"

"You're getting closer!" Alan joked.

Bryan had convinced Misty to come with him and Alan to see the car for herself. As he had put it on the phone, this way she could get up close and personal with the Cataluna. She could finally understand his obsession.

The Cataluna sat in its usual spot. The far corner of the lot away from the other cars. The three of them circled the car in the moonlight. When they talked, the chilly air froze their breath in little white clouds.

To Bryan the car seemed almost alive. Magical. He half expected the headlights to follow them as they moved around it, the way the eyes in paintings sometimes seemed to do.

"Misty, check out the chrome work," Bryan urged, showing her. "Notice all this detail? Isn't that awesome? You don't see that on most cars."

"Uh-huh."

Doesn't she realize this car is one in a million? Bryan thought, annoyed.

Misty stuffed her hands deeper into the pockets of her suede jacket. "I'm sorry," she muttered, "but this is a little boring."

Bryan glared at her.

She made a face back. "We saw the car. Now what? Can't we go to a movie? Oh, I forgot." She gave Bryan a genuinely sympathetic glance. She knew she had goofed. "We were going to rent a movie, right?"

Bryan didn't know why he had insisted they save money tonight. Stuffed into the back of his sock drawer, inside his Coke can safe, he now had two hundred extra dollars. Two big ones that he hadn't had yesterday.

No! The stolen money was for one purpose, and one purpose only, Bryan told himself. The Cataluna. If he spent any of that money on trivial stuff, like a date, it would somehow make his crime more wrong.

"I know," Misty said. "How about that new Wino- na Ryder film with Keanu Reeves? Have either of you guys seen that? I think it's out on video by now."

Alan moaned. "I rented it last night, and I hated it. I got so bored I ate a whole bag of Reese's Pieces. I broke out so bad. I should have saved time and glued the candy directly to my forehead." He kicked a pebble.

Bryan stiffened. The rock had come dangerously close to hitting his precious car.

"Come on, let's go to the movies," Alan said. He glanced at Bryan. "My treat."

"Great!" Misty cried, clapping.

"Uh, you two go," Bryan told them. "I have to go somewhere."

He noticed Alan and Misty exchanging glances.

"You sure, man?" Alan asked.

"Yeah."

Misty pulled him aside. "Bry," she said softly, concern clouding her big green eyes.

"What?"

Alan wandered away, letting them have their privacy. He started drumming on the top of the Cataluna with both palms.

Bryan tried to concentrate on what Misty was saying. But he kept wanting to yell at Alan to cut it out.

"Please come," Misty begged.

"No. I can't. I told you. I have to go do something."

Misty stared down, watching her white Reebok sneaker scuff the pavement. When she glanced back up, Bryan could tell she felt hurt. "Go where?" she asked in a low voice.

Once he had started lying to Misty, the lies came faster and faster. "Somewhere," he mumbled.

"I don't get it!" she exclaimed. "First you cancel out on our dance date. Now you can't even rent a movie?"

"Yeah, I'm really sorry, but—"

"But what?"

He felt all squirmy inside. Why couldn't she accept the fact that he had to go? He thought about reminding her that she promised he never had to make excuses to her. What happened to that?

"I'm really worried about you, Bryan. You've been acting strange. You're not yourself. I'm serious."

He gazed across the street at the dark windows of a muffler shop that had closed. "I'm just tired, I guess. Come on. Let's get out of here."

Alan drove them away from the lot. No one talked much.

Finally Alan pulled up in front of Bryan's house, a small green clapboard that badly needed repainting. He hated when his two rich friends came anywhere near the place. So embarrassing.

"Bryan," Alan cautioned, "time to reconsider, dude. Seriously. This is the point of no return. You leave now and you leave me alone with Misty. And as we all know, there's no way any woman can resist me for long."

Nobody laughed.

"Sorry," Bryan muttered. "So what are you guys going to do?"

"Without you?" Alan replied. "We'll probably just sit and cry!"

"Seriously."

"Well, I still want to go to the movies." Alan turned to Misty.

"Sure," Misty agreed, staring straight at Bryan.

Why am I throwing Alan and Misty together? Bryan asked himself. But he trusted Alan. Alan would never try anything.

Bryan climbed out, then leaned in the window to kiss Misty goodbye. "I'm fine," he told her. He could tell she thought something was wrong.

"Hey," Bryan added cheerfully, "next Saturday night I'm going to make this up to you in a big way, okay? I mean, that date we talked about for tonight? It won't be like *anything* compared to next Saturday night. And that's a promise."

"Bryan," she said, "you don't have to—"

But he stepped back before she could finish her sentence. "Thanks for the ride, Alan," he called. Then he turned and trotted up the walk to his house. He stepped inside and quietly shut the door behind him.

He hid in the dark by the window. He could see Alan and Misty in the car, watching the house, talking. About him, he knew.

No sound came from inside the house. Who knew where his parents were? Good.

Alan pulled away and Bryan stepped back outside.

He hiked for almost thirty minutes, heading away from his neighborhood. To a better neighborhood. He reached Canyon Road. Here the houses all had two-car garages and two cars in them.

The kinds of houses with cash lying around. More Ben Franklins waiting on glass coffee tables.

Easy pickings. As easy as last time.

The first two houses he passed had lots of lights on. He spotted someone moving around in a bedroom window.

He strolled for a couple of blocks more before he found a house with all the lights off. He started across the lawn.

Spotlights flashed on.

He stood frozen.

The lights clicked back off. Motion detectors, he realized. Had anyone seen him?

He hurried back to the sidewalk, then jogged into the shadows. He crossed the street. Then stopped when he found the perfect house.

A large Victorian loomed before him. Its castlelike turrets lifted high into the darkness. A porch wrapped around the right side.

No lights on in the entire place. No cars in the large garage. Best of all, a broken streetlight in front of the house.

Standing under a large tree, Bryan felt safe. Such total darkness would cover his actions from the entire world.

He strode up the driveway. Through the open, pass-through garage. Into the backyard.

No light on in back, either. No dogs barking. Perfect.

The huge house towered over Bryan like a giant sleeping monster. Bryan almost lost his nerve. But he forced himself to continue.

He climbed the steps to the porch. His shoes rasped noisily against the cement.

Then he pulled open the porch door. Slowly. Slowly.

He set one foot inside the porch.

A gunshot rang out.

Bryan uttered a cry—and went flying backward.

chapter
16

*B*ryan landed on his back on the cement porch. His head hit hard. Pain throbbed through his body.

Then he heard laughter. Screams. Then another gunshot. And another.

The sounds came from a TV.

But if someone watched TV inside the house, that meant . . .

He scrambled to his feet. His head rang. His back throbbed. The shot had been fake, but the fall had been real.

He hurried back through the garage and out to the street. The TV had warned him that someone was home. If it hadn't been for some fake gunshot in a TV movie, he might be in jail right now.

He cursed himself. I can't believe I'm actually robbing houses, he thought. Car or no car, it's wrong.

Car or no car.

Bryan had tried to explain to Alan and Misty how much the car meant to him. But he couldn't make them understand.

One or two more thefts and he'd have the down payment. After that he could swing the monthly payments with his salary from the flower store. He'd go back to being himself, Bryan Folger.

And what is so great about that?

He stood on the sidewalk. He had every right to be there. No one owned the sidewalks. But he felt so scared and guilty. He wouldn't have been surprised if a cop car zoomed down on him and a police officer arrested him for being outside late at night.

As he waited for his breathing to return to normal, he stared across the street at the house opposite the big old Victorian. Smaller. No car in front. No light in the windows.

Those signs fooled you once already, he reminded himself.

But what are the odds that two dark houses would have people inside?

Rubbing his aching neck, he crossed the street. Then he glimpsed the mailbox. Pieces of mail stuck out of the box's metal mouth. The mail hadn't been taken in for several days.

He remembered something else he could check,

something from his newspaper delivery days. He trotted up the walk to the porch. Yes! He found several rolled-up papers on the doormat. A few more lay around the side of the porch where the paperboy had tossed them.

These people had gone away without canceling the paper. Or asking their TV-watching neighbors to collect the papers for them.

Dumb, dumb, dumb. They had set out a welcome mat for Bryan.

He tried the garage door. Locked. He stood on tiptoes and peered through the small windows. Empty. He circled around to the side of the garage. But he discovered a metal fence.

No problem. He climbed up and over. Step one.

In the darkness he made out a small kidney-shaped swimming pool covered with a blue tarp. Wet leaves lay on top.

A small patio had been furnished with ugly metal lawn chairs. The chairs seemed to light up as they caught the silvery glow of the crescent moon.

He tried the back door. Locked, of course. It's not going to be *that* easy, thought Bryan. They don't give you the money. You have to use your head.

He found a rock. He slipped off his black sweater and wrapped it around the rock. He struck the rock against a back window. Once. Twice. The glass cracked. Pieces fell inside the house.

Too much noise, Bryan thought. Even with the sweater. He waited for a long time, watching the windows of the house. Checking the houses he could see on either side.

No lights came on. No alarm sounded. Safe.

Tell that to his body.

His head felt as if it might come flying off! He could feel his blood pumping wildly. *Crazy! Crazy!* His pumping blood carried the word to all parts of his body.

His hand trembled as he reached through the hole in the window. His hand scraped against the jagged glass. He swore.

Bryan found the lock on the sash and turned it. Carefully he eased his cut hand back out of the hole. He studied the wound. Not too bad. A small price to pay.

He slid the window up. Hoisted himself through. Then he slid the window shut behind him.

I'm in. Yes!

He crept forward. Hands groping blindly in front of him. He should have brought a flashlight. On TV all thieves carried long black flashlights and wore black ski masks. Now he knew why.

Something hard sliced into his knee. He grunted.

His eyes adjusted to the darkness. He'd bumped into a heavy wooden desk chair.

The chair stood in front of a rolltop desk. He started to slide up the top. It stuck. He forced it open.

He pulled out papers from the cubbyholes inside, holding them up close to his eyes. Envelopes. Stamps.

He thought about turning on a light, but he didn't want to take the chance.

You've been lucky. Don't push it, he told himself.

Besides, he liked being in the dark. He could pretend he wasn't really here.

He made his way out of the study into the living room. Then up a wide front staircase.

Upstairs, he found the master bedroom. A huge bed with a wooden frame. Tall hulking dressers, His and Hers, one on either side. Bryan started with His.

He explored the top of the dresser with his hands, holding each discovery close to his eyes. He found a few scattered coins, a shoehorn, a seashell, other worthless objects.

He opened the top drawer. Underwear. He started to close it. Then he remembered his own underwear drawer at home. And the Coke can safe hidden in back.

He reached deep into the drawer. Worked his fingers through the layers of cloth and the furry balls of rolled-up socks. Until he touched something cool and smooth.

A box.

You are a genius, Bryan! he told himself. He had never paid himself such a high compliment in his life.

He pulled the box out and held it up to the trickle of light from the bedroom window. A cigar box.

He opened it. Whistled softly through his teeth.

Stacks of bills rubber-banded together.

Bryan had a recurring dream throughout his life. In the dream he found a shiny silver dime lying by the side of the road. Then another, then another. Pure joy filled him as he collected those free coins.

For the first time life matched his dreams. Here was all the money he needed to buy the Cataluna. And then some.

What if this is a dream? What if I wake up and all

the bills have disappeared the way those shiny dimes always did?

He reached his hand slowly into the box. He gently felt the thick wads of cash.

Definitely real.

He lifted the first pile out of the box.

Two strong hands grabbed him from behind.

chapter

17

*"F*reeze. Police," a voice said softly, but firmly.

Lights flashed on.

Bryan dropped the box and the money.

The hands yanked him away from the window and shoved him up against the wall. His nose smashed into the wall. He could taste the blood trickling down into his mouth.

Large, strong hands moved over his body. Slapping at pockets. He had no weapon. He hadn't even remembered to bring a flashlight.

Someone pulled his hands painfully close together behind him. He felt cold steel slip around his wrists. *Click. Click.* Handcuffed.

Hands turned him around. He blinked. Two cops, a man and a woman stood there. Both big, both in bulky blue uniforms. The man stood farther away. His gun drawn. The woman had grabbed him, frisked him, cuffed him. Both cops appeared shocked.

The female officer cursed. "How old are you, kid? Twelve?"

Bryan gulped for air. He thought he might faint. Or throw up. He couldn't speak.

"So stupid," the other cop growled. His walkie-talkie blared. He pulled it off his belt and reported Bryan's capture.

"H-how did you know I was here?" Bryan choked out as they led him out of the bedroom.

It's so unfair, Bryan thought. He had been so careful. So quiet. He had come so close. He had held the money in his hands.

"The alarm, kid," explained the woman cop. "You set off the alarm."

Dazed, Bryan stumbled outside. The cop car sat parked out front. Its red and blue rack of lights flashed crazily in the darkness. The female cop pushed his head down roughly and shoved him into the back of the patrol car.

"What alarm?" Bryan asked. Stupid question, Bry, he told himself. You're being arrested. What does it matter how you got caught? "I didn't hear any alarm." His voice shook.

"It rings at the station," the cop replied as she climbed into the front of the car. "It's a silent alarm."

Jail, Bryan thought. I'm going to jail.

* * *

103

On the day of Bryan's appearance in juvenile court, his father shaved carefully. Unusual enough. But then Mr. Folger put on his best clothes. A chocolate-brown, three-piece suit that Bryan never even knew his father owned. Mr. Folger appeared pale. He didn't speak a word all the way to court.

Bryan's dad often picked on him for nothing. Now he had the perfect reason to yell at him and didn't.

That made Bryan feel even worse. The pain on his father's face hurt Bryan more than any insults his dad could throw at him.

During the hearing, Bryan stared at the floor. He felt too ashamed to meet anyone's gaze. He tried to estimate the number of tiles in the floor. Anything to distract him from the woman police officer's testimony.

Finally the judge asked him to stand for sentencing.

Here it comes, Bryan thought. He glanced up at the judge's stern expression. He doesn't like me. He's going to send me to juvenile prison. Bryan shifted nervously from foot to foot.

"Since this is your first offense, and since you are still a minor, I'm going to suspend your sentence," the judge informed him. "I do not want to find you in my courtroom again, Bryan. You only get this chance once."

I'm not going to prison! I can't believe it.

"In addition," the judge continued. "I'm going to assign you three months of community service. It's an experimental program, Bryan, designed to help young offenders such as yourself. As part of this program, you'll be assigned a guidance counselor. You'll have to check in with the counselor twice a week."

I'm free, Bryan thought. He hurried out of the courthouse with his parents. He wanted to run. He wanted to shout for joy.

Then he saw her. Bryan felt his stomach flip.

Misty. Standing by the courthouse steps.

What could he say to her?

"Bryan!" She threw her arms around his neck.

He let her hold him. Bryan stood stiffly, hands at his sides. At last she pulled away. She raised her eyes to his.

I've really disappointed her now, Bryan thought.

"I came to say goodbye," she told him.

He hadn't been expecting that. He didn't know what he had been expecting, but not that. The last thing he needed to hear today. "Goodbye?"

She blinked quickly. Trying not to cry. "My parents. They won't let me go out with you anymore. How could you do it, Bryan? How *could* you?"

Bryan shrugged helplessly. He couldn't really explain. Not even to himself. He just knew he had to have the Cataluna.

Even now. With Misty saying goodbye to him. The sick expression on his dad's face. His mother's tears. He wanted that car.

He needed the Cataluna.

* * *

The Folgers' phone rang. It had been ringing all day. Bryan didn't want to talk to anyone.

"Bryan?" His mother knocked softly on his locked bedroom door. "It's Alan on the phone. He's been calling all afternoon."

"Tell him—" He wanted to say, "Tell him I died." But he stopped himself. His mother would start crying again. Bryan didn't want to make her feel any worse. "Tell him I'll call him back in an hour, I promise."

"That's what you said last time, Bryan."

"I promise," he repeated dully.

After his mother's footsteps padded away, Bryan pulled down the window shades all the way to the bottom. Blocked out the fall sunshine. He sat on the edge of his bed, hands clasped tightly around his knees, rocking himself back and forth.

Icy air seeped through the cracks in the window frames. But Bryan felt perspiration roll down his forehead.

If a surgeon cut open his brain right now, Bryan knew they would find a single picture.

A picture of a sleek white car.

He held out for twenty minutes more, then charged out of his room and bounded down the stairs. He opened the front door as Alan raised his hand to knock.

Instead of knocking on the door, Alan knocked softly on Bryan's forehead. "Hey, Bry. I've called you a million times."

"Alan, hi. I can't talk right now, I'm really late and—"

Bryan pushed past him, hurrying away down the walk.

"Bryan!"

Alan spoke so sharply that Bryan had to stop. He stared back at his friend.

"I need to talk to you, Bryan."

"Sorry. I'll have to call you later."

He climbed onto his bike. The bike wobbled once as Bryan pedaled up over the grass between sidewalk and street, then bumped down onto the pavement. He picked up speed. He didn't turn back.

He had to see the Cataluna.

"And two packs of gum come to—"

He punched a button. The register rang up the total and popped open. "Two fifty-nine."

The heavyset woman reached for her purse. She didn't open it. "Listen," she said. "Maybe you can help me. I want to get something for my friend's daughter. She had a baby girl. But I couldn't find anything I liked. Can you recommend something?"

Bryan gave a wide smile. His old Happy Burgers smile. He'd been using it ever since he started doing his community service work at the hospital gift shop. "I like those teddy bears over there." He pointed. "The ones that say 'I was born at Shadyside Hospital.'"

"Oh, those *are* cute."

Actually, they are pretty dopey, Bryan thought. Who would feel good about a gift someone had obviously picked up at the last second in the hospital gift shop? So bogus.

He watched the woman pick up several bears, checking the prices. Whenever she glanced back his way, he gave her the smile. But his mind had drifted far away. Two miles away to be exact.

Denny's car lot.

A week had gone by since he'd seen it last.

What if someone bought the car?

One house. That's probably all it would take. Rob one house.

And this time he would have experience. He knew what to do. He'd case out the place for several days. Learn the people's schedules. And—

"Bryan?"

"Yeah."

His supervisor, Mrs. Glenn, put a hand on his shoulder. "I have to run out for a moment. Can you watch the store by yourself?"

"Of course." He gave her the smile. She smiled back.

"Oh," he called, glancing at the clock. "I'm off in ten minutes."

"I'll be back before then. But if you need to go, make sure the door locks behind you and put the sign up."

"Right."

She left him alone.

Standing at the register.

The open register.

All the bills lined up for him in their neat little slots.

THE EVIL MOON

I'm volunteering here, Bryan thought. Not making a cent. I lost my job at the florist shop.

Three hundred dollars in the register.

Maybe more.

The faces on the bills smiled at him.

They whispered in his ear.

Take me. Take me.

chapter

18

Bryan's hand slipped into the register.

He kept his eyes on the customer. She stood checking out the rack of teddy bears. No one else in the store.

Without glancing down, he removed most of the cash in the ten-dollar slot. He stuffed the bills into his pocket. Then he lifted the tray and grabbed the twenties stored underneath. Shoved them into his pocket, too.

He started to close the register drawer. Then remembered the customer. "Ma'am? I'm going to be leaving soon."

"Oh, I'm sorry," she apologized. "I can't seem to

make up my mind. I'm terrible about decisions. Do you ever have that problem?"

I have bigger problems, believe me, thought Bryan. He started to sweat. He stared at the front door. He wanted to be out of there before Mrs. Glenn returned.

Sirens of alarm blasted in his brain. Mrs. Glenn would know right away that he took the money. She knew he was doing community service work because he'd been caught stealing.

This is crazy, Bryan thought. Completely crazy.

Too late to put the money back.

Come on. Come on! he silently urged the customer. Hurry!

At last she came up to the register carrying two teddy bears. Both pink. Identical.

"I think I've narrowed it down to these two. Which one would you take if you were me?"

I'd take either one and take it fast—because otherwise I'm going to end up in jail. "That one."

"This one? Are you sure? Why?"

Why? "I don't know. It's got cuter eyes."

The customer glanced from one bear to the other and back again. I'm going to scream, Bryan thought.

Finally she said, "Okay, I'll trust your judgment." She set the bear on the counter and reached for her purse.

He rang up the sale. "That's twenty-one thirty-nine." The customer put a twenty on the counter. She pulled a crumpled single from the bottom of her purse.

"Now, let me see . . ." the customer began. She

fumbled inside her purse for change. She counted out two dimes, then a nickel. Then came a bunch of pennies. "These pennies make me crazy," she said. "They fill up your pockets. I'm always trying to get rid of them."

She counted up to twenty-six cents. "That's close enough," Bryan told her. He scooped the change off the counter and dumped it into the register without even bothering to sort it into the proper trays.

He tossed the teddy bear into a plastic bag along with the woman's gum, roll of Life Savers, and Bic pen. He came around the register. Handed her the bag. And walked her to the door.

"It's nice to see a young man working," she remarked.

"Thank you."

He pulled the "Open" sign off the door. Stuck on one with a cutesy drawing of a guy in traction. It read "Back in a minute. Please be patient." He pulled the door shut behind him.

The woman blocked his way. "It's been a pleasure doing business with you, young man."

"Sure."

He managed one last smile. A cold drop of sweat raced down his cheek. He could feel dampness around the edge of his collar and under his armpits.

He moved past the woman and across the wide hospital lobby. The revolving doors spun before he could step inside.

"Bryan, hi! What a pleasant surprise!"

Mr. Palmer beamed at him. The elderly man lived two doors down from Bryan's old house. Where they used to live before his dad lost his job.

Mr. Palmer's smile vanished suddenly. "But why are you at the hospital? I hope no one's sick."

"No, no, no, nothing like that," Bryan reassured him, trying to move past the old man. "I'm doing some volunteer work here. But I've got to—"

Mr. Palmer gripped Bryan's elbow with fingers like claws. "How are your parents these days? They don't come by to see me. Your father owes me a game of chess. Tell him that, will you?" He poked Bryan in the chest. "Is he afraid he'll lose?"

"Yeah, I'm sure that's what it is. But listen, Mr. Palmer, I'm really in kind of a rush."

"You could come by, too, you know. Wouldn't kill you."

"I will, I promise."

Mr. Palmer stared down and frowned.

What does he see?

Bryan glanced down, too. The tips of several green bills poked out of his pocket. He stuffed them back inside.

"What grade are you in now?" asked Mr. Palmer. "You're a junior now, unless memory fails me. Right?"

"Senior. This is my senior year."

"Ah. Then it's time to think about college. But I don't have to tell you that. I'm sure you've already got it all planned out. A bright boy like you. What colleges did you apply to? Let me hear the list."

"Mr. Palmer—"

"Now, now, don't try to weasel out of it."

Bryan turned and gazed across the lobby. Mrs. Glenn stepped around the corner.

"Mr. Palmer," he said. "I swear I'll come by and see

you real soon. You can beat me at chess and everything." He gently but firmly removed the old man's hand from his elbow. "But right now I've got to go. Really."

Bryan plunged into the revolving door, banging his head hard before he started the door moving.

Yes! I'm out!

His heart pounding, he ran to his bike. Jumped on and started pedaling furiously.

You're going to get caught, he told himself over and over. *You're crazy.* Bryan pedaled faster.

He skidded to a stop in front of his house. Dropped the bike on the lawn. Slammed through the front door. Climbed the stairs to his bedroom two at a time.

He dumped his underwear drawer out on his bed. Frantically he twisted off the secret screw-top lid of the Coke can safe. He pulled out all his money. He didn't have to count it. He knew he had enough money now.

He grabbed the money and flew down the stairs. Back out to his bike.

"The car is mine!" he shouted as he pedaled to Denny's. "It's mine! Mine!"

The two miles seemed to take forever. Finally he bounced over the sidewalk in front of the car lot. He leaped off the bike, letting it clatter to the ground.

He turned to the spot where the car was kept.

"No!" he wailed. "No! It can't be!"

The Cataluna was gone.

part

5

West Hampshire Colony
1698

chapter

19

Adam Hatchett's face twisted into a sneer of hate. He raised the musket to Catherine's chest. And pulled the trigger.

Catherine gasped.

She stumbled backward.

But the shot never came.

"Let that be a warning to you," Adam Hatchett spat in a low voice. "The next time the musket will be loaded. I will shoot you myself, Catherine. I swear it."

Catherine inched away. Mr. Hatchett strode down the steps after her. Still aiming the musket at her chest.

It is not loaded, Catherine told herself. But she could not stop shaking.

"You cannot sleep in this house tonight, Bad Luck Catherine," he growled. "No more bad luck in this house. The colony council has banished you. They will come for you at dawn. If you are still in the village, they will hang you."

Her father's cold face horrified her almost as much as his words. There was no love here for her. Perhaps he had never loved her. The thought made her knees buckle.

"Go!" he ordered sternly.

She turned away from him and stumbled into the darkness. Tears flowed freely down her face.

Dawn. They would come for her at dawn. How far could she get on foot before then?

Not far at all.

She knew she must run. But she felt too exhausted.

She stumbled to the shed. The old gray door hung open. She peered inside. On a row of metal hooks hung the saddle and tack for their workhorse, Mary.

Mary had died of a strange disease. The poor beast had been hit by the cursed bad luck that everyone blamed on Catherine.

Catherine turned the corner of the shed and stopped. Braced herself against the splintery shed wall. So tired, she thought. I need to rest. Only for a moment.

She slumped to the ground and curled up into a ball. Like a sleeping cat.

I will rest for a moment.

After all, I have until . . .

Dawn.

* * *

"Dawn," Catherine whispered when she awoke.

Then she heard the voices.

"I bet she is as far as the colony of Covington by now. At least she is if she knows what is good for her."

"She is nowhere around this house, that I will promise." Her father's voice.

"I almost hope she stayed. It would be a pleasure to hang her for the bad luck she brought to all of us."

"Come," called another angry voice. "Let us check the house completely. I trust you, Adam, but she may have hidden here without your knowledge. Noah, you search that field. Martin, check the barn. You, Luther, check Adam's shed."

The shed. Where Catherine listened in growing terror.

She sat up. Her heart pounded rapidly, as if she had swallowed a live creature and it struggled to escape from her chest.

She slept too late.

Too late to escape.

Now they were here to hang her.

chapter

20

Catherine forced herself to her feet. On trembling legs, she started to run.

If only she could reach the woods. If only she could reach Gwendolyn's cabin.

She raced behind the neighbor's house. Panting hard, she spun around.

No one behind her. She crept past the next house. The next.

Townspeople gathered everywhere. Talking in clusters of threes and fours. Men with guns. Men on horseback.

She inched along the back wall of a house, ducking down each time she came to a window. With every passing moment the sun rose higher and higher. Glaring down at her like an angry eye.

No storm clouds today. Her bad luck continued. The heavens provided her enemies with clear skies to help them hunt her down.

She darted through the town stable. The horses whinnied as if scolding her. Only a few houses more before she reached the woods.

Catherine spotted three women standing on the porch of the Harkness house. As they talked they turned their heads this way and that, searching for her.

She stepped back quickly into an open doorway. Noah Foster's house.

Perfect, she told herself. Everyone searched for her outside. No one would check inside a house.

"What are you doing here?"

The soft voice clutched at her heart. She whirled around.

A redheaded boy stood across the room from her in his white nightgown. Charles Foster. Nervous, sweet, he had often been kind to her. One of the few.

Then she remembered something else about this boy. She had hit him in the head with a rock.

"Charles." She smiled at him. Put a finger to her lips. And backed toward the open window.

He stared at her blankly. What is he thinking?

"Please," she whispered softly. Would he take pity on her?

Still that blank face. Those staring eyes.

Catherine swung one leg over the window, pulling her skirt out of the way.

And then the boy began to scream. "Bad Luck Catherine! Bad Luck Catherine!"

Footsteps. Shouts.

Catherine uttered a cry. She jumped out the window. Fell. Scraped her shin hard.

She ran for the woods. Ran as fast as she could, her hair streaming behind her. Holding her skirts high.

A shot rang out. She felt the heat as the musketball whizzed past her head.

Bark flew as the shot gouged a huge hole in the trunk of a pine tree. That hole could have been in my back, Catherine thought.

She ran harder, head down, waiting for the next shot to burn through her with incredible force and pain.

A shot roared out. Missed her.

She stumbled through the woods. The pine trees guarded her now. Hid her from view.

One of her shoes fell off. She did not stop. Her foot began to bleed.

Gwendolyn would know how to rescue her.

"Gwendolyn!"

She caught sight of the cabin. Pain screamed up through her foot with every step. She dragged herself to the cabin's open door.

"Gwendolyn!" The word ripped out of her.

No reply.

She staggered into the cabin.

Stopped.

Stared at the floor.

Her stomach heaved.

Blood. Pulpy red flesh. Bones.

Catherine's breath caught in her throat. The room spun as she recognized what she had found.

The remains of a cat. A cat that had been skinned.

Catherine groaned, low in her throat.

Then she saw the fur. Silver and black. Hanging from the mantel over the fireplace like a trophy. The cat's dead eyes stared out blankly at Catherine.

She gently removed the hide from the wall. Stroked the silver and black fur.

"Mother? Who killed you, Mother?" Catherine murmured. She buried her face in the cat's soft fur.

She wanted to give Gwendolyn a proper burial. But she knew she could not stay in her mother's cabin a moment longer. They would find her here.

She gently set down the fur. Then she ran. Deeper into the forest. With no idea where to go.

Catherine usually loved dawn in the woods. Birds awaking, singing in the trees. Sun splashing on the soft blanket of pine needles that covered the forest floor. But now the peacefulness of her surroundings only added to her terror.

She crossed a stream, slipping on the mossy rocks.

Every part of her ached.

Then a wonderful thing began to happen. She began to feel her mother's spirit. She felt as if Gwendolyn guided her. Told her which way to turn. Gwendolyn was trying to save her!

She burst into a clearing.

"Oh!" Her hand flew to her mouth.

She faced the most amazing creature.

A monster?

She backed away.

But the monster did not stir. Or roar. Or charge. It stared at her blankly with two huge eyes.

She circled around the creature. Silvery and white. Smooth as snow. And so sleek. She wanted to run her hand along the monster's smooth body. But felt too afraid.

Then the creature's eyes began to glow with a bright yellow light. Catherine gasped. The lights in the creature's eyes faded slowly away.

The monster stretched out as long as her parents' woodshed. But stood not half as tall. It had four black wheels and clear windowpanes all around. Through those panes she found another wheel of sorts. And two rows of seats, red as blood.

In the distance she heard the barking of dogs. Men shouting.

"She has been here!" someone cried.

She turned toward the voice. The men had reached Gwendolyn's cabin.

She turned back to the white monster. She knew one thing. Her mother had led her here, to this clearing, for a reason. Her mother would never want the townspeople to find the white machine. Gwendolyn meant it only for her.

Catherine scrambled up a grassy embankment on all fours and disappeared back into the woods. Even if they caught her, at least she could lead them away from the magical white being.

She ran as fast as she could. The pain throbbing in her foot. With every step, needles seemed to pierce her body.

THE EVIL MOON

She heard the men coming closer. Their rapid footsteps crashed through the brush.

She stopped, gasping for breath. Which way should she turn?

Before she could decide, three large men burst out of the woods and grabbed her.

part

6

Shadyside
1995

chapter

21

Bryan stared at the empty space where the Cataluna had stood. Then he burst through the glass doors into the sales office. The young salesman stood helping a customer fill out some forms.

"Where is the Cataluna?" Bryan demanded.

The salesman stared at him. "What?"

"The Cataluna! Who bought it? Who?"

Bryan charged across the office toward the man.

"Excuse me, young man, I'm in the middle of—"

"Please, just tell me!" Bryan pleaded. "The Cataluna. I *have* to know."

The salesman made a sound of disgust. "That friend of yours bought it."

"Friend? What friend?"

"The guy who always came with you to drool over it. Now, if you'll excuse me—"

Alan? Bryan thought. No! Alan couldn't do that to me. Could he? Alan knows how much that car means to me!

Bryan stormed out of the office. He ran back to his bike. He rode to Alan's house in a blind rage. How could he? How could he? How could he?

Parked in Alan's driveway stood the sleek white sports car with chrome racing stripes. The car appeared even more beautiful off the lot. "No!" Bryan shouted. "No! The Cataluna is mine!"

Alan came trotting out of the garage. "Hey, Bryan. I just tried to call you."

"Give me the key!" Bryan shrieked. He grabbed Alan by the neck of his sweater.

"Get off, man! What's the matter with you?" Alan jerked away.

"Give me the key!"

"No."

"What do you mean, no?"

"No. No way!"

Bryan's chest heaved. "Give me the key. Now!"

Alan actually smiled. "You heard me."

With a cry of fury Bryan pulled back his fist and smashed Alan in the face.

Alan's head snapped back.

Holding him by the sweater, Bryan hit him again. Again.

Alan's hands came up to block the blows. Then he sank to his knees. His head drooped. He let out a groan.

Bryan locked both hands together like a club and swung at Alan's jaw with all his might.

Alan's head jerked to the side. He sagged onto his back, his body twisted at an unnatural angle. Blood poured from his nose and mouth.

Bryan bent down and shook him. "The key!" he shouted. "The key!"

Alan didn't move. Bryan released the sweater. Alan dropped to the pavement. And didn't move.

Bryan reached his hand roughly into one of Alan's front jeans pockets. A wallet and a stick of Wrigley's. He threw them on the pavement. Next pocket. A bunch of keys on an Orioles keychain. "No!" Bryan yelled.

He kept digging. Yes! He grabbed the key to the Cataluna. The white mother-of-pearl molded around the key gleamed at him like treasure.

Breathing noisily, his blood pulsing at his temples, Bryan strode toward the Cataluna. He flung open the car door and jumped inside. He pulled hard on the door, but it closed with a quiet click.

Bryan started the car. Stepped on the gas. He hit the brakes with a screech. Stopped inches away from one of Alan's outstretched hands.

He snapped the car into reverse and backed down the driveway. He turned right, then roared away.

In his rearview mirror he noticed a black BMW pulling up at Alan's house. Alan's mother climbed out. She dropped her groceries and ran up the driveway to Alan.

Bryan drove faster.

The car handled great.

He drove down Fear Street. What a thrill! The Cataluna is mine!

"Bryan, you're finally here."

The girl's voice. The one he heard during the test-drive.

"Welcome back, Bryan."

He reached out to flick the radio off.

But it was off already.

He heard a little chuckle. *"You sure have kept me waiting, Bryan."*

"Who are you?"

"Oh, never mind about that. The important thing is that you're here. And now we're going to be together. Forever!"

chapter
22

Bryan felt a chill of fear.

He hit the brakes.

The car sped faster.

He stared down. Did he hit the wrong pedal? No. Maybe the brake fluid had leaked out.

The Cataluna shot down a dead-end street. At the end a small colonial house loomed into view behind a white picket fence.

Bryan stomped on the brake pedal, pushing it down to the floor.

The car lurched forward. It crashed through the picket fence, pieces of wood flying in all directions.

The car jolted hard, bouncing over the lawn.

The girl's voice laughed in Bryan's ear.

"Who are you? Where are you?" he shrieked.

Gripping the wheel with both hands, he aimed the speeding car through the garden on the side of the house. Shot toward the back door of the house behind it.

A man in a gray overcoat stepped out the door carrying a bag of garbage.

Bryan spun the wheel—and hit something hard.

A metal trashcan flew into the air, bounced against the side of the house. The man dived out of the way, screaming.

Bryan flew down a sloping lawn and over a curb. Back on the street. He spun the wheel hard. The tires screeched in fury as he struggled to keep the car on the road.

The car veered left. Up another lawn.

Faster.

"I told you, Bryan. We're driving forever!" the girl's voice cooed. *"You and me."*

"Stop!" Bryan pleaded. "Why won't it stop?"

Time to bail, Bryan thought.

He fumbled for the door handle, lifted it, then shoved his shoulder against the metal.

His shoulder bumped hard. The door didn't budge.

Locked. One hand on the bouncing wheel, Bryan jerked up the little button.

Before he could try the door again, the button shot back down, locking itself.

Gleeful laughter from the girl.

"Stop laughing!" he cried. "Who are you? Who?"

Bryan screamed as the car scraped metal on both sides. He rocketed through a narrow space between a fence and the side of a house. Sparks shot up around him.

He spun onto the back lawn of a house. Two small kids played in a leaf pile while their father raked.

Bryan hit the horn.

No sound came out.

The father screamed, threw the rake, dove to his left. The kids didn't move. Frozen in surprise.

The car tore through the leaf pile, sending up a shower of yellow and brown and red.

Bryan stared back. The two kids popped out from under the leaves.

The car bounced through an alley. Into another yard. Into the black cavelike mouth of an empty garage.

Bryan closed his eyes. Prepared for the crash.

With a splintering crack, the car burst out the back of the garage.

Back on the street. They took the next corner so sharply that two of the tires lifted high into the air.

"Wheeeeeee!" the girl cried.

The Cataluna bumped back down. Fishtailed. Then zoomed ahead.

Straight for a group of high school kids playing touch football in the street.

I can't stop, Bryan realized. I'm going to run them down.

But the kids managed to fling themselves to safety.

All except one. A dark-haired boy holding the football.

Pounding on the silent horn, Bryan uttered a long scream of horror.

Something slammed against the side of the car.

Bryan turned. Yes! I only hit the football.

It stuck to the side mirror.

Strange.

Bryan stared at the shape more closely. What was stuck on top of the football?

The guy's hand!

Bryan choked. Started to vomit. Swallowed it. The girl laughed merrily.

"Please, whoever you are. Let me go. I'm sorry! Please. Slow down. I'm begging you!"

"Aw, that's sweet."

He couldn't breathe. No air in the car.

He pressed the power button to lower the windows. They didn't move.

Streets flew by. Terrified faces. He heard blasts of horns. Brakes screeching.

Then it all blurred. Bryan wheezed. White spots flashed in front of his eyes.

I've got to go back to Alan's, he told himself. He had stolen the car from Alan. If he could return it, maybe he could undo this horror.

He spun the wheel. For once the car obeyed. "Got to get back to Alan's . . ." he gasped.

Everything started to fade. Can't . . . breathe . . . he thought. Can't . . .

He opened and shut his mouth. No sound came out.

His body felt as if it were collapsing in on itself.

He heard a loud roar in his ears.

Then a heavy blackness washed over him.

chapter

23

The Cataluna stood in Alan's driveway. Unscratched. Shiny. Milk white.

Only the front fender bore a mark. A small red spot that blistered and puckered in the bright sun.

Police swarmed around the car. Alan and Misty watched from the bottom of the driveway.

The police hadn't moved Bryan yet. He still sprawled inside the car.

Burst blood vessels had turned his face reddish-blue. A terrifying silent scream twisted his features. His blank eyes bulged. His dead hands still gripped the wheel.

"Oh, Alan!" Misty cried, turning her face away.

Alan wrapped one arm around her shoulders. He let her cry against his sweater.

She turned back to the car, staring with tear-filled green eyes.

"Don't," Alan said softly.

She didn't listen. Alan knew what she was thinking. They owed it to Bryan to watch this. To watch the police remove his body.

"Do they have any idea—?"

"What happened?" Alan finished her question for her. "No. They say he drove around town like a total maniac and nearly killed a bunch of people. I found him here in the driveway." Alan nodded toward the gruesome scene.

For the first time since she had arrived, Misty seemed to focus on Alan. She saw the bloodstains on his face, the bruises. "Alan, what happened to *you?*"

"I tried to stop Bryan from driving off," he told her with a grim shrug. "But Bryan wouldn't take no for an answer."

The officers finally pried the car door open. Bryan's hands made a hideous creaking sound as they were pried off the wheel.

Misty moaned.

"Come on." Alan tried to lead her away.

She wouldn't move.

More sirens as an ambulance arrived. A lot of good an ambulance is going to do for Bryan now, Alan thought.

"I don't get it," he said. He felt hollow inside. "What happened to Bryan? He was such a great guy."

"You were the great guy, Alan," Misty replied softly.

"Me?"

"Yeah. Getting your parents to buy the car for Bryan for a birthday present."

"One more week," Alan muttered. "I wanted him to wait one more week, so I could give him the car the way I planned. So stupid. I should have handed him the key right away."

"No, you shouldn't. See what happened?" She shook her head sadly. "You were a good friend, Alan. If only he'd given you a chance to explain. If only . . ." Her voice broke.

She took Alan's arm. They walked closer to the car.

"Hey, what's this?" Misty asked.

She reached down and ran her finger over the red spot on the front fender of the white car. Shaped like a crescent moon, the red spot felt burning hot.

Misty jerked her hand away. "Weird."

"I'll tell you one thing," Alan declared. "I never want to see this car again." He took her hand. "Come on, Misty, I'll walk you home."

She allowed him to lead her away.

"Goodbye, Bryan," she whispered.

part

7

West Hampshire Colony
1698

109

chapter
24

*T*he men dragged Catherine facedown through the woods. Her legs and belly scraped over rocks and branches and thorns.

Catherine tried to squirm away. But she had no strength left.

"Get her on her feet," someone commanded.

Hands grabbed her by the hair. Fingers dug into her arms. Tore her skirt. They pulled Catherine to her feet.

She could barely stand. Her legs felt weak as a rag doll's. Blood leaked down from her forehead and into her eye, making it hard for her to see. But she knew she stood in a clearing. A clearing ringed with townspeople.

More of them arrived every moment. Their faces grim. Grim and eager at the same time.

"We will wait until everyone is here," ordered a familiar voice.

She turned and squinted at Edmund Parker, Joseph's father, dressed in his Sunday best.

Then she noticed something else. She shivered.

A large tree stood at the edge of the clearing. A tree with a thick, strong branch jutting out to the side. She knew this tree. In the colony they had a name for it.

The hanging tree.

Two young men huddled beneath it, a thick, knotted rope in their hands. One man slung an end of the rope up and over the branch.

Soon they had fixed the noose. It hung down, swinging gently.

One of the men set a wooden crate under the noose. A platform of death.

Catherine's body went limp. She sank to her knees. She wept. "Please," she sobbed. "Please!"

No one spoke. They all watched her with unforgiving faces.

She could sink no lower than this, she thought. She almost wished they would hang her and be done with it. If so many people hate me this much, she thought, I don't want to live.

But then she remembered her mother.

She heard a distant hiss. The wind in the trees?

No. Gwendolyn. Her poor dead mother.

Catherine wanted revenge on those who killed her mother. She had to live.

But what chance did she have?

Edmund Parker nodded to the men nearest her. They picked her up.

Catherine began to kick and buck.

More hands joined in the struggle. They stood her on the crate. Slipped the noose over her neck.

Her legs buckled again. The men had to hold her up.

"Look at the coward," someone murmured.

"Silence," commanded Edmund Parker. He gazed at her solemnly. "Catherine Hatchett," he declared, "you have been found guilty by the town council. You have worked your black magic upon us, and you have almost destroyed us.

"We gave you fair warning, Catherine Hatchett. We told you to leave this place and yet you did not. You stayed and now you must endure a harsh fate.

"I beg you, Catherine, in the few moments left to you before you go to meet your Maker, confess your sins."

Catherine's head tilted to one side. Edmund Parker's words sounded as though they came from miles away.

"Confess!" chanted the spectators. "Confess!"

Catherine opened her lips as if to speak. But no words came.

What sins should she confess to? They had decided to hang her when she had done no wrong.

"Confess, Catherine!" Edmund cried. "Who knows the trials and tortures that await your soul in the world to come? If there is to be any hope for you, you must unburden yourself now, my child. Confess!"

He pressed his hand against the red crescent moon on her forehead. "Bad Luck Catherine, Catherine of the Bad Moon, for the last time, I beseech you. Use your final moments on this earth to confess!"

Catherine turned her head, slipping away from his hand. She felt the harsh noose, thick around her neck.

She caught glimpses of familiar faces. William Parker. Adam and Martha Hatchett. Faces filled with hate.

Like a mirror, her face filled with hate as well. She could not speak. She felt her face turn red. She spat.

The white gob hit the shoulder of Edmund Parker's stiff black cloak.

A gasp of shock rose from the ring of onlookers.

The gasps turned quickly into cries of rage.

Edmund Parker's face darkened. "Very well, Catherine," he told her. "Your sins will be on your head."

Then he yanked hard on the noose, tightening it around her throat. She began to choke. Her hands flew up to the noose, tugging at it desperately. Trying to free herself.

Edmund Parker raised his hand high in the air.

The crowd grew silent.

He slashed his hand down.

The crate flew out from beneath her.

Catherine swung down.

A shock of pain. Catherine saw a flash of bright red.

Her legs floated above the ground.

She swung slowly from side to side.

The rope tight around her neck.

She had no breath left.

No breath at all.

chapter
25

Catherine shut her eyes.

And remembered.

I do not need to stay a girl.

I have powers. The powers of my mother.

She willed herself to change.

Change. Change. Change.

She felt her body draw in. Felt the rope loosen as she grew tiny. Tinier.

She changed into a squeaking white rat.

Edmund Parker's mouth gaped open with shock.

Then she leaped.

Into his open mouth.

She jammed her head deep into his throat. Pushed herself farther and farther inside.

Blocked the air from reaching him. Blocked his windpipe.

Choked him. Choked him.

She could feel his hands frantically grasping at her hindquarters.

She burrowed deeper into his throat.

Good. Good. Good, she thought, listening to his dying gurgles.

Good. Good. Good.

Helpless and stunned, nobody moved. They watched Edmund Parker's face turn bright red, then purple.

Dangling out of the man's mouth was the tip of a pink tail.

Shaking off his terror, William Parker ran forward. He grabbed for the tail hanging out of his father's mouth.

Too late.

Edmund slumped to the ground.

He lay silent and still.

No one in the crowd spoke.

Everyone knew Catherine had been born under a bad moon. But watching her transform before their eyes filled them with fear and awe.

William pulled his father over onto his back. His father a dead weight in his arms.

With an angry cry William reached for the rat's tail.

But the rat worked its way out of his father's mouth.

William grabbed for the rat with both hands.

Leaping over his outstretched fingers, the rat dropped to the ground and began to run.

It raced in a fast zigzag through the crowd. People screamed and jumped out of its path.

When it cleared the crowd, the white rat transformed again. It rose up as a tall white horse with a flowing white mane. The horse galloped away, effortlessly moving through the trees. And then it disappeared.

William Parker watched the horse disappear. He shook his fist with anger and grief.

"You have escaped today, Catherine!" he cried in anguish. "But I shall find you. You have murdered my father and my brother. But I am still alive. And I will have my revenge!"

Behind him, the townspeople watched in stunned silence. William's shouts faded into the chill air.

epilogue

*E*ven though I had not yet seen the white car, my destiny was sealed that day three hundred years ago.

My quest to avenge my father and brother led me through horror after horror. Horrors so difficult to recall—horrors that will have to be told another time.

Yes, I am William Parker. And my journey began on that day that I swore to hunt down Catherine. The day that I first spoke her true name, her birth name. The name everyone in my colony felt too terrified to speak.

On that day, I vowed, "I shall never rest until I kill you. Catherine. Cat of the Moon. *Cataluna!*"

About the Author

"Where do you get your ideas?"

That's the question that R. L. Stine is asked most often. "I don't know where my ideas come from," he says. "But I do know that I have a lot more scary stories in my mind that I can't wait to write."

So far, he has written more than fifty mysteries and thrillers for young people, all of them bestsellers.

Bob grew up in Columbus, Ohio. Today he lives in an apartment near Central Park in New York City with his wife, Jane, and fourteen-year-old son, Matt.

Discover the DARK SECRET in Book #2 of THE
CATALINA CHRONICLES

THE NIGHTMARES NEVER END . . . WHEN YOU VISIT

Next . . .
THE CATALUNA CHRONICLES
BOOK #2: *THE DARK SECRET*

They came from different centuries. Different worlds. But the same evil force could destroy both their lives.

William Parker lives in the West Hampshire Colony in the year 1698. He is determined to destroy Catherine Hatchett. The girl with the strange red crescent-moon birthmark on her forehead brought bad luck to his colony. The animals died. The crops failed. And then Catherine killed his father and his brother.

William must stop Catherine—before she kills again.

Lauren Patterson lives in Shadyside in the year 1995. She is afraid her stepsister Regina is Shadyside's hit-and-run killer. Ever since Lauren and her stepsister got the sports car with the red crescent moon on the fender, Regina has been acting strange. Wild. And Lauren has found blood on the car's bumper.

Lauren must stop Regina—before she kills again.

How could an evil be powerful enough to travel three centuries through time?

Discover the *DARK SECRET* in Book #2 of THE CATALUNA CHRONICLES.